C000003811

SLOW RIDE HOME

A MATURE-AGE CHRISTIAN ROMANCE

JULIETTE DUNCAN

A SUNBURNED LAND - BOOK 3

FOREWORD

HELLO! Thank you for choosing to read this book - I hope you enjoy it! Please note that this story is set in Australia. Australian spelling and terminology have been used and are not typos!

As a thank you for reading this book, I'd like to offer you a FREE GIFT. That's right - my FREE novella, "Hank and Sarah - A Love Story" is available exclusively to my newsletter subscribers. Click here to claim your copy now and to be notified of my future book releases. I hope you enjoy both books! Have a wonderful day!

Juliette

PROLOGUE

$\mathcal{T}$here was nothing like Goddard Downs at dusk. Vibrant reds, oranges and yellows gave way to deep blues and purples as the clouds reflected the light of the disappearing sun. It was a sight Joshua Goddard knew well. One he'd taken pleasure in for as long as he could remember. Watching the sun set with his mother had been one of his favourite pastimes. But not tonight. Tonight, the once sweet sight filled him with bitterness.

The only sure thing in life was change, his mother used to say. However, that didn't make change any easier. Life was constantly making choices for him, removing him from the equation while expecting him to accept the consequences of choices he had no part in making. He didn't ask for his mother to die, or for his father to marry a woman he didn't know. He'd taken no part in his older brother, Julian, becoming head over the cattle station, yet, he was expected to be the dutiful son and accept everything in his stride. *But how could he when it meant his life was not his own?*

His mum would have understood. She always understood, but she was no longer there. She hadn't been for years, and no matter how many passed, it still didn't seem real that she was no longer alive.

"What are you thinking about?" his cousin, Sean, questioned as he brought his horse to a stop alongside Joshua's.

Sean's reputation was less than stellar. Everyone knew it. Unlike others, however, Joshua was willing to overlook his faults. Sean had some good qualities, though they were often difficult to appreciate.

Joshua leaned forward in his saddle, crossing his hands casually over the horn. "Nothing important. Just remembering."

Sean grinned. "Something good?"

Joshua pondered the question. The expansive sky over Goddard Downs once filled him with wonder, but lately, it had been losing its lustre in his eyes. He exhaled a deep breath. "Once."

"Don't worry, mate. Soon, you and I will be out of here and the wide-open world will be at our feet. No more restrictions or Julian looking over our shoulders. We'll be our own men again like we were in Alice Springs." He thwacked Joshua's chest with the back of his hand.

Joshua chuckled. He remembered that trip. One week had quickly turned into three for him and Sean as they enjoyed everything the rodeo had to offer. Sean was there for the women and parties, while Joshua had basically gone along for the ride. Until he met a girl who'd made his time there more memorable than he could ever have imagined. A grin spread across his face at the memory of the gorgeous blonde who'd wound her way around his heart.

"See, what did I tell you? That smile alone assures me you'd rather be anywhere than here. Who wouldn't? This place is dullsville compared to rodeo life. Excitement every day. Notoriety. Not to mention the ladies." Sean smirked mischievously. He didn't *only* think of women, just mostly. It was something Joshua was used to.

In Joshua's case, the rodeo wasn't that for him. Rather, it was a way of proving himself amongst others. Setting himself apart. Feeling special. Julian would never be caught dead on the back of a bull or a bucking bronco. He was too sedate for that. Too stable. An ideal son.

Again, a hand struck his chest as Sean studied him curiously. "Where are you, cuz?"

"Right here. Where else would I be?" Joshua turned his horse away to conceal his face. He didn't need his cousin recognising the lie in his expression. He was usually able to hide his feelings, adopting a blank stare that had become his signature, but not with everyone. Sean was one of the few who could see through him.

"Don't think I don't know what's bothering you," Sean called from behind.

His profile appeared in Joshua's periphery, but Joshua refused to look at him. "What?" he asked gruffly.

"The wet season's coming. I know what that does to you. You start thinking of your mum, and then you start withdrawing from life. Happens every year."

Joshua turned at his cousin's comment. While Sean wasn't

the most discerning person, he often noticed what others didn't. His cousin was his best friend. The guy who was always there with a plan for fun. A plan to take his mind off his troubles. Still, there were some things he couldn't help with. This was one of them.

Swinging his gaze to the darkening horizon, Joshua's mind filled with images of his mother. She'd been the rock of the family, the glue that kept them together. She'd made him feel he was an integral member of the family at Goddard Downs. Now, with all the changes, he felt lost, like he didn't belong anymore. Sean couldn't understand the depth of those feelings, the powerful weight that pressed down on him each year as the anniversary of his mother's death approached. Joshua simply replied, "Yeah, I miss her."

Sean remained silent as they led their horses home under the darkening sky. When the homestead came into view, Joshua's chest tightened, and by the time the horses were stabled and the pair were walking towards the house, he felt as if he couldn't breathe. Stopping at the bottom of the stairs, he said, "Go in without me. I'll be right behind you."

"What's up?" Sean frowned.

"Nothing. I just need to deal with something. I won't be long. Tell Dad and the others I'll be right there, but don't wait for me."

Sean's brows drew further together but he didn't delve. Instead, he nodded and disappeared inside.

There were no walls falling in on him, but Joshua felt as if his lungs could get no air. It would be worse inside. It would be stifling, and not just from the heat. If only he could leave the cattle station. Be his own person. Live his own life. *But could he?*

Sighing, he pulled his phone from his pocket and dialled Stella's number. She rarely answered, but today he hoped she would. He put the phone to his ear. With every fibre of his being, he prayed he'd hear her comforting voice on the other end.

STELLA MARTIN CROSSED the yard to the paddocks to check on the two heifers that were due to give birth to their first offspring any day now. Indigo was a small cattle station close to the town of Kununurra, and her family's home for the past twenty-five years, but not for much longer. The family's livelihood stood on a precipice since the announcement of the live cattle ban. The export of live cattle was the foundation of their entire business. Their lives. They were trying other options to sell their beef and to stay afloat, but given how slow things had been for them in the past few years, there was no way they could afford the changes.

She tried not to think of the dire situation they were in as she approached the paddock where the cows were stabled. Their head hand, Daku Henderson, was filling up their feed boxes.

"How are we doing, Dak?" she asked as she pulled her sandy blonde hair into a bun and held it in place with the hairband from around her wrist.

"So far so good, Miss. I think we should see our new calves

in a few hours," he replied, flashing a smile as the dying sun shone on his chocolate-hued skin.

Standing beside him, Stella cast her gaze over the cows. She was tall for a woman, with sun-kissed skin, high cheekbones, and a strong, slender frame from years of working on her family's cattle station. She leaned against the paddock rail and smiled. "Great."

She hoped the new calves would arrive soon. She had plans for the following day and didn't want to put them off longer than she already had.

Shuffling his feet on the dry earth, Daku lowered his gaze before lifting it slowly to meet hers. "I have to tell you something, Miss."

Stella frowned. "What is it, Daku?"

"I…I found a new place." His dark eyes watered, his gaze barely holding hers.

Stella groaned as her shoulders involuntarily drooped. Although many of the station hands had already left, Daku, along with a few others, had remained, but it seemed that was about to change. How many would still be there by the time the rainy season came? The thought worried her. They needed every hand they could get during that critical time.

She forced a smile, but inside her heart was breaking. Daku had been with them for as long as she could remember. Unlike many cattle stations where the hands were just that, at Indigo, the hands were family. Stella had been raised with these men, women, and their children. She had no siblings, but their children were like her brothers and sisters. Each day, when someone else informed her of their departure, it was like she was losing more of her family.

"When do you leave?" she asked, forcing her voice to remain steady.

"Two weeks. Gina and I wanted to give you more time, but our new bosses need us right away or not at all."

Stella nodded. "I understand. You can't lose this opportunity and risk the job. I get it."

"We feel terrible. But your father hasn't paid us in three months. We've stuck around out of loyalty, but that doesn't cover the bills. We know when things turn around he'll make good on his promises, but we can't wait."

Stella's brows arched. She knew things were difficult, but her father hadn't mentioned not paying the hands for so long. What else was he hiding? "Dak, I understand. You and Regina have to think of your family, of Rianna, Koa, and Tarka."

The Henderson children were all under the age of ten and had been born at Indigo Downs. Now they were leaving, and Stella already felt the loss. "Be sure to tell me how to contact you. I wouldn't want to lose touch just because you've moved."

Nodding, Daku smiled. "Of course. You are family, Stella. We will never lose touch. Tarka wouldn't allow it. He loves you so much."

Tears stung her eyes. The little boy had stolen her heart from the moment he'd made an appearance into the world four years earlier. "We'll miss you all, Daku." She stepped forward and gave the man a hug.

They lingered for several seconds, the pain of the family's coming departure already filling her with an inexplicable feeling of loss, but it was for the best. She had no idea when things would turn around. She couldn't expect Dak and his family to stay until then, no matter how much she might want them to.

When they separated, he said, "I know you won't want to consider this, but if things don't change soon, you'll need a job. I heard through the grapevine that Goddard Downs' large animal vet is retiring. It could be an opportunity for you, Miss. I've never met a vet who cares as much as you do. You'd be excellent for the job, and I'm sure with your experience, they'd pay you well."

Stella smiled wistfully. "Thanks for thinking of me, Dak, but I can't leave Mum and Dad. They need me, especially when things do turn around."

He nodded. "I thought you'd say that. Still, I had to let you know. It's not public knowledge yet that the vet's retiring, so it would give you an edge before they start advertising. The rains will come soon and they'll need the vet before then."

"That's true, but as I said, I can't leave my parents."

"You are a good daughter, Miss. Your father's lucky to have you."

"Thank you, Dak. And I'll speak to my father and ensure that somehow you get paid what's owed to you."

Dak's eyes welled. "Thank you, Miss. I appreciate that."

Stella trudged back to the house, kicking up red dust that lingered in the air. Her heart was heavy. What did the future hold? She knew she shouldn't worry. She trusted God to look after her and her family, but there were moments when despair hovered like a heavy, dark cloud, and this was one of them.

Her father's truck was parked outside the house. He'd left early that morning without a word and she'd been wondering all day where he'd gone. It was out of character for him to disappear like that.

"Mum? Dad?" she called as she hurried up the front timber steps. The paint had peeled off them, and the house itself was in general disrepair, but it seemed her parents didn't notice anymore.

She headed down the hallway to the back of the house. Her parents were standing together in the small office, their expressions grave.

Her heart pounded. "Mum? Dad? What's wrong?"

Her mother's cheeks were damp. She sniffled and turned away. "You tell her, Jim."

A cord tightened around Stella's heart. "Tell me what?"

"We've lost it," her father choked. "I met with the bank today to plead for more time to pay the loan, but they wouldn't budge. They're foreclosing on us, Stell. We have two weeks to get everything cleared out."

Stella could barely draw breath. "What?"

"We haven't paid the mortgage in six months. I was hoping the deal with Emcorp would save us, but they weren't interested in our cattle. There's nothing left." He raked his hand across his balding head and slumped into the chair. "I hoped the bank would come good, but they offered nothing. I can't blame them. I can't think of any way to turn things around, and if I can't, how can I expect them to?"

Stella slipped a comforting hand onto his shoulder. She hated seeing this man who'd raised her and put everything he had into providing for her and her mum so defeated. "Why didn't you tell me?"

"We didn't want you to worry, love." He covered her hand with his and squeezed it.

"What are we going to do?"

He drew a deep breath. "Your mother and I have decided to move back to Cootamundra. We still have friends and your mother's family there, and your grandmother's house is empty. It'll take time to get it liveable, but one of your mother's friends has offered to let us stay in their guest house for a while."

Stella couldn't believe what she was hearing. They were giving up so easily? *They were willing to give up more than three decades of hard work just because of some money issues?* Yes, the bank was taking the station, but things could still turn around. They could get it back, they just had to try. "Dad, you can't mean this."

Her mother stepped closer and placed a hand on her shoulder. "I know this is difficult for you to hear, Stella, but it's over. We've done everything we can, but it didn't work. Your father did his best. It just didn't happen for us this time."

"That was because I didn't know. I could have helped." Stella sounded petulant, like a child who couldn't accept being told she couldn't have something she wanted, but she simply couldn't believe what she was hearing. It was craziness. Her parents were going to leave all this behind and move to Cootamundra? Unbelievable!

"What could you have done that I didn't?" Her father pinned her with his gaze.

She couldn't answer. She didn't know what she could have done, but she would have tried harder. There was no way she would have given up. Fumbling for words, she contemplated what could be said to make things better, to make her parents believe that things could turn around. Something that would encourage them. Praying silently, she searched for words that might turn their despair to hope but came up empty. When her phone rang, she didn't look at it. There was nothing in the world more important than what was happening in this moment. Whoever it was, they didn't need her more than her parents.

CHAPTER 1

*M*aggie would never tire of the quiet mornings at Goddard Downs. The sky was not yet lit as her eyes opened, a smile immediately lifting her cheeks as she felt the comfortable weight of Frank's arm around her waist. Looking over her shoulder at her sleeping husband, she thanked God again for blessing her with such a man. Never could she have imagined that at this stage of her life she could be so happy. *The glory of this latter house will be greater than of the former, saith the Lord of hosts: and in this place will I give peace.*

She slipped from beneath his arm, careful not to wake him. Hovering at the foot of the bed, her smile lingered on the man who had turned her latter days into something infinitely better than the former. Sometimes she wondered what her life would have been like if she'd met Frank when she was younger, but the thought of life without Serena and Jeremy was inconceivable. Frank would say the same about his children. The choices they had made brought them to the state of happiness they now enjoyed. How could she ever regret that?

Life seemed perfect. Serena and David's newfound faith was a source of comfort, and the impending arrival of their baby gave delight every time Maggie thought of the new life Serena was carrying. However, the good news didn't end there. The stress of the live cattle ban was a faint memory at Goddard Downs. The decision to move to a tourism venture had been a wise one and they were reaping the rewards, with everyone benefiting. Olivia's marketing plan was nothing short of genius, producing a consistent flow of visitors since opening their doors, and now, with the rainy season approaching, they had enough remaining visitors to ensure the season would end on a high note.

The steps of a good man are ordered by the Lord: and He delighteth in his way. Though he fall, he shall not be utterly cast down: for the Lord upholdeth him with His hand. I have been young, and now am old; yet have I not seen the righteous forsaken, nor his seed begging bread. He is ever merciful, and lendeth, and his seed is blessed.

Turning to leave, Maggie's progress was stopped by the sound of Frank's groggy voice. "Where are you going, my love?"

"To get breakfast."

"Can't breakfast wait? Come back to bed."

She chuckled at the hangdog expression on his face. "Frank…you're incorrigible."

"I know. But indulge me."

She honestly didn't mind indulging him. Their honeymoon

might be over, but their love had continued to deepen, and there was no place she'd rather be than in his arms.

She caved. How could she resist a man as handsome and loving as Frank Goddard? "Just a cuddle, then I need to get moving." She slipped into bed and snuggled into his arms.

Until recently, Frank had spent every waking second thinking of the station, but since Julian, his eldest son, had taken on more of the responsibility for its running, Frank had more time on his hands. Not that Maggie minded. Spending time together brought them both great joy, but she sensed he still hadn't fully adjusted to not being in charge. It was something that would come slowly, and he needed to develop other interests. She had her gardening and writing, but his whole life had been wrapped up in the station. They couldn't spend their whole lives in bed.

Nudging her chin with his thumb, he brushed her lips gently with his. "I love you, Maggie."

Her lips parted, and just as he was pressing harder, her phone rang, the ringtone immediately alerting her to the identity of the caller. Serena. Maggie laughed. "Our children know when to call, don't they?"

Frank groaned and rolled onto his back. "Yes, they do."

She patted his chest comfortingly before sitting up and grabbing her phone from the nightstand. "Hi, Serena."

"Mum." Serena's voice was laced with tension.

"What is it?" Maggie replied, immediately alert. Was the baby coming?

"What's better? Cloth or disposable nappies? I don't know. This baby is going to be here soon, and I have no idea what I'm doing."

Maggie stifled the urge to laugh. Becoming a mother was an emotional event, even without the assistance of pregnancy hormones. She recalled crying at television ads when she was pregnant with Serena. Now, her daughter was experiencing the same things.

"It doesn't matter, sweetheart. Whatever suits you. It isn't a big deal."

"Yes, it is. I'm supposed to be his mother. I'm supposed to know what's best for him, but I can't even decide on something as simple as this."

Serena's tearful response touched Maggie deeply. Her daughter wasn't sure of her capability of being a mother, and doubt was eating away at her, but Maggie knew without question that Serena would be a great mother—she simply couldn't see it yet. Maggie gripped the phone and uttered a quick prayer. *Lord, please give me the right words to say to Serena. Words that encourage her and boost her confidence. You know how uncertain she is.*

Stepping outside onto the small balcony, Maggie eased herself onto the cane couch. "Serena, no mother knows everything, but you'll learn. When I had you, I didn't know what I was doing. Even when I had Jeremy, I couldn't predict what would happen. You can only pray and ask God to guide you as you do your best. God doesn't give us more than we can handle without providing the means."

"I know. I pray about it. You're confident. David's confident, but no matter what I do, I can't get myself in that place. I never imagined myself as a mother. I just don't feel prepared. I've read the books, but I still don't feel ready."

Maggie chuckled at her daughter's tirade. They'd had the

same conversation nearly all the way through her pregnancy. And Maggie had nearly always said the same thing back. "Few women feel ready, especially with their first child. Having a baby is a life-changing experience. No one is prepared for that fully. But you have so much more information available than I ever had. You simply have to believe in yourself. You may not be able to see it, but I know you'll make a wonderful mother."

"Emma said the same thing." Serena's tone had subdued.

"And she's right. I've seen you with Sebastian and Chloe. You're so good with them, sweetheart."

Serena protested. "That's different. They aren't my children. If I make a mistake, I can give them back and Emma will fix it. If I make a mistake with this baby, then I have to live with it for the rest of my life, knowing I ruined everything for him."

Maggie winced. It was quite distressing to hear her once confident daughter, who'd been the European correspondent for the NABC before the terrorist attack that had left permanent scarring on her face and a good part of her body, sound so unsure of herself. "Serena, don't listen to that voice that's telling you that. It isn't true. What does the Bible tell us? I can do all things..."

"...through Christ who strengthens me." As Serena finished the verse, a wave of joy filled Maggie's heart. Serena might not think she had it in her, but as long as she let God lead her, she would be fine.

"Do you believe what you just said?" Maggie asked.

There was a tentative silence punctuated by a sniffle before Serena answered, "I want to. But it's not easy."

"How's David doing?"

Frank poked his head through the open door, mouthing his intention to prepare breakfast while she finished her conversation. Maggie mouthed back a thank you before he disappeared.

"He's been wonderful," Serena replied. "He's come to every birth class with me, and we pray together. He understands how I feel."

Maggie was so thankful that David had stuck it out with Serena, despite all her efforts to push him away. The transformation in them both since they'd given their hearts to the Lord had been no less than amazing. She was so glad he was there for her daughter. Maggie had always believed he was a good match, although it took Serena more time to see that. Now, they were making a family together. It was more than she could have hoped for. God had a way of doing more than she could ever imagine.

"You have nothing to worry about," she said. "You have a strong man at your side. Just keep your chin up and ask God to give you the eyes to see this situation for what it is, a gift. This baby is a blessing, and God chose you to be his mother. That means you have everything it takes for the job."

There was a moment of silence. Serena blew her nose. Finally, she replied, "I know you're right. I can do this. I went into far more dangerous situations than this as a journalist. I can be a mother. I can decide what nappy is best for my baby."

Maggie chuckled. "That's my girl. Of course you can."

Serena sounded more certain, but there was still a hint of doubt. "I know I can do this, but I'd feel better if you were here. Could you come to Darwin for the birth? I know it's a lot to ask, being so far away, and I know there must be a lot to do there with the rainy season coming, but I'd love it if you could find some way to come."

Maggie's initial response was to say yes, but it wasn't that simple. She wasn't a single woman any longer; she had to think of Frank and the family at the cattle station. "I'd love to be there. Let me talk to Frank and I'll let you know. Is that okay?"

"Yes. I understand. Let me know as soon as you can."

"I will, sweetheart. Go and get some rest. I'll call you as soon as Frank and I have talked."

"All right. Bye, Mum, I love you."

"I love you too, Serena."

Maggie ended the call and headed to the kitchen to talk to Frank. They'd already discussed travelling to Darwin to see the baby before the wet season set in, and while she had no doubt he'd agree to her being there earlier to support Serena, they needed to talk about it.

He was standing over the stove, spatula in hand, when she reached the kitchen. He looked up from the sausages that were sizzling in the pan. "Is everything okay?" His clear blue eyes looked deep into hers.

Maggie nodded. "As well as can be. Serena's still worried about being a good mother." She stepped around the counter and slipped her arms around his waist, resting her head against his back. "She said she'd feel better if I was there when the baby comes."

He turned and faced her. "I think you should go. In fact, I'll come with you."

"Really? We could be away for a month or more, not just a couple of weeks."

"I know."

Maggie stretched up and kissed him on the cheek. "You're a good man, Frank Godard."

He grinned. "You'd better believe it."

"You are *so* incorrigible!"

"But you love me." He lowered his mouth to hers and brushed her lips with his.

"I sure do," she mumbled as she reached behind him and turned the stove off.

CHAPTER 2

*D*espite Serena's misgivings, Maggie had every confidence in her daughter's ability to be a wonderful mother. In time, she prayed Serena would see that too. The Lord had spared her life, brought her and David together, and now was blessing them with a child. He had a plan for her daughter, even if Serena still could not see it.

Maggie took satisfaction in that thought as she ran her hand over the soft quilt she was working on. Serena and David's baby was a blessing to them all and she wanted to be sure they both knew that. The baby's birth was still six weeks away, but whatever day he chose to make his appearance, Maggie would be ready to welcome him.

Frank was fortunate to have his children and grandchildren so close. Now she lived at Goddard Downs, a twelve-hour drive from Darwin, she missed the ease of visiting Jeremy and Emma and looking in on Chloe and Sebastian, and she was very much looking forward to seeing them when she returned to Darwin for the new baby's birth. In the meantime, there were still a few items she could get for the gift basket. August would be here soon, and two months after, the rains would be upon them, blocking road access to the property.

A smile grew on her face as she perused the online offerings. Shopping for her grandchildren was such a joy. She found the items to complete the gift for her new grandson and ordered a few toys for Chloe and Sebastian as well. She couldn't wait to see their faces when they saw the gifts and didn't care if their parents thought she was spoiling them too much. She couldn't help being a doting grandmother.

Closing her laptop, she stretched. There was nothing left to do at the cabin. She'd already cleaned and tidied before going online to shop. Perhaps Janella could use her help in the kitchen. After all, today wasn't a usual day at Goddard Downs.

The changes on the cattle station meant a lot of changes to the family's dynamics. Family meals, though still important, were sometimes not attended by everyone. Joshua and Sean were often away taking guests on the overnight cattle drives, and she and Frank were spending more time at home together. They'd even started exploring the area and had taken a few overnight trips, although Frank's idea of camping seemed rather different from hers. He was happy with a swag and a billy over an open fire. She would have at least liked a tent and a gas cooker. But they were learning to compromise, and so long as they were together, she didn't really mind roughing it a bit. They'd started discussing taking a longer trip when the time was right, and she insisted they upgrade their camping gear before they left. Frank promised they would, and she was happy with that.

With all of these changes, any opportunity for the entire family to gather together was important, and today's meeting would hopefully satisfy that need. Having everyone together would make Frank happy, and what made him happy made her happy, too.

After strolling the short distance to the main house, she followed the mouth-watering aromas wafting down the hallway to the kitchen where Janella, Frank's daughter-in-law and Julian's wife, was preparing a large meal for the lunch meeting. Sweat dripped from her brow as she hovered over several pots. Sasha, her twelve-year-old daughter, sat at the table feeding her cousin, William, while his older sister, Isobel, danced around them playfully.

"Hi there," Maggie greeted as she entered the room, setting her water bottle and bag on the counter.

Janella looked up, a smile on her face as she returned Maggie's greeting. Sasha also looked up and smiled, but instead of speaking, five-year-old Isobel ran to Maggie and stood before her, arms folded and wearing an unhappy frown. "Grandma Maggie, will you play with me? Sasha's giving William his lunch and Aunt Janella's busy cooking. There's no one to play with me."

Chuckling, Maggie bent down and patted her head gently. "I actually came to help your Aunt Janella with her work, but I promise that once we're finished, I'll play a game with you. Does that sound good?"

Isobel's lips puckered, but finally she nodded. "Okay. So long as you promise. Grandpa says once you make a promise you have to keep it. You must always be a person of your word."

Maggie nodded. "Your grandfather is very wise. I believe the same thing."

Isobel grinned and ran back to the table where Sasha was having a hard time feeding her cousin.

"Did I hear you say you came to help?" Janella asked, wiping her brow with her arm.

"I did. With everyone so busy, I thought you could use a hand."

"Great." Janella smiled and handed Maggie a large wooden spoon. "A helping hand is always appreciated. You can keep an eye on the stew and rice while I chop more vegetables to steam."

Maggie stepped up to the large industrial stove, uncovered the pot of stew and stirred it gently. Janella was a remarkable woman to cook for so many, plus manage all her other responsibilities on the station without neglecting her family. Maggie had first glimpsed the resilience of the women who lived in this remote area of northern Australia when she'd been commissioned to prepare articles for the Country Women's Magazine two years earlier. That was when she met Frank.

She had so much still to learn about her new family. In time, she hoped to understand them all. They'd welcomed her as part of their family, and though she could never replace Esther, Frank's first wife who'd drowned seven years earlier, she did want to do her best for them and help them as a mother would.

Sasha watched over William and Isobel while Maggie helped Janella. Sasha was twelve, and with her olive skin and warm, brown eyes, she was already developing into a beautiful young woman.

It wasn't long before the dishes were complete, and Maggie and Janella sat talking over mugs of tea while they waited for the rest of the family to arrive. The table was already laid, thanks to Sasha, and as promised, Maggie indulged herself in two games of hide-n-seek with Isobel before Sasha took her cousins outside to play.

Janella smiled wistfully. "It seems that Sasha was Isobel's age only yesterday. Now look at her. Soon she'll be as tall as me, if not taller. And Caleb will be leaving for boarding school in Darwin soon. Where did my babies go? They've grown up so quickly."

Maggie could remember the feeling of loss when first Serena, and then Jeremy, left home. At Goddard Downs, however, the separation happened at a younger age. Maggie's children were in their late teens when they flew the nest. Caleb was only fourteen. Not that he was leaving for good, but she imagined it would be heart wrenching for Janella, and Julian, to send him off to school when it was so far away.

She sipped her tea. "You women are remarkable."

"What do you mean?" Janella frowned.

"You do so much on the station, most of the time without much thanks. Then you stand by and watch your children leave when they're so young. You're very strong, Janella."

Janella shrugged. "It's just what we do. We don't know any different, and we have each other."

It was a sentiment Maggie had heard at most of the cattle stations she'd visited for her story. Although she'd garnered a wealth of information, she'd only scratched the surface. Perhaps now, being part of a cattle station herself, she could delve deeper into the life she was writing about and the women who were the subject of her articles.

She nodded. "Yes, the family support here is amazing."

"And you're part of that family now." Janella smiled warmly. If there was anyone on the station who made Maggie feel that sentiment was true, it was Janella.

"Thank you. And that means so much to me."

"I mean it. It might not be said often, but we're all thankful to have you here. Frank hasn't looked so happy in years, and the children love having you as a grandmother. I know it must be strange for you sometimes, but I want you to know that I'm always here."

Maggie set her cup aside and placed her hand over Janella's. "Thank you."

"You're more than welcome." Janella's smile was warm and genuine, and a deep sense of contentment flowed through Maggie.

Loud voices outside interrupted the moment.

"I don't care what you thought. I expected it to be done the way I told you. That's it!" The voice belonged to Julian. Maggie met Janella's gaze and winced.

"Come off it, Julian. The matter was handled and everything worked out. Is it really important how it was done?"

Maggie sat back as Janella sighed heavily. "Here we go again."

Maggie's head angled, her forehead creased. "What do you mean?"

"Julian and Joshua. They're at it more than ever these days. Ever since Frank gave Julian more responsibility, they bicker like cats and dogs."

"I thought they got on okay."

Janella shook her head. "Not for years. Since Esther passed away, the friction between them has grown, but lately, it's become almost a daily occurrence."

Maggie was speechless. She was sure everyone on the station got along well. She'd not seen signs of turmoil beneath the surface, and Frank had never said anything about it. *Perhaps he doesn't know...* "Is Frank aware of it?"

Janella grimaced. "We try to keep it from him. He's happy, and he's taking things easier now he has you. He shouldn't have to be the intermediary between squabbling siblings. Julian and Joshua are old enough to work out their own issues. And I wish they would. I'm getting tired of the arguments."

Janella rose to her feet and placed her mug in the sink and started to wash it. Maggie couldn't tear herself from the argument that was continuing in the next room. Something had to be done. Frank would be there any minute to join them for lunch. He didn't need to hear this. It would only upset him and make the lunch tense.

Maggie stood and placed her mug on the sink. "Perhaps it's not my place, but I think I'd like to speak to them. They can't keep up like this. Their father will be here soon."

Janella took Maggie's mug and rinsed it under the tap. "I hope you have better luck than I've had."

Maggie gave a hopeful smile. "I'll do my best."

She couldn't help but think of Cain and Abel as she paused at the door between the kitchen and dining room. Arguments between brothers could become severe and destroy a family. She was sure the arguments between Julian and Joshua weren't that bad, but nonetheless, it was better dealt with sooner than later. If she could help them resolve the matter without having to involve Frank, it would be for the best. Her husband was pleased that things were finally settled on the station and that his family was a happy unit. She didn't want that equilibrium upset.

Hovering at the door, she uttered a quick prayer. *Lord, please give me the right words to say. I don't want to make things worse, but something has to be done to stop these two bickering.*

She drew a deep breath and knocked quietly before stepping into the room. "Julian. Joshua. Is everything all right? I could hear your argument from the kitchen."

Julian was the first to reply, his voice quickly adopting a happier tone. "I didn't know you were here, Maggie. I thought Janella was the only one in the house."

"I was helping prepare lunch. The commotion surprised me and I thought I should figure out what was happening before your father arrived. I expect him at any moment."

Julian's gaze swung to Joshua. The latter remained silent, arms folded, eyes narrowed.

"If there's a problem, I'd like to help." She gulped. It was obvious she was overstepping. Intruding, even.

"There's no problem," Julian snapped. "Just brothers having a disagreement. Nothing you need to worry about. And it's not something Dad needs to worry about, either."

Maggie's gaze swung to Joshua. The younger brother remained silent, his gaze avoiding both hers and Julian's. He was a mystery. Julian was devoted to the station and displayed copious amounts of responsibility. Sometimes he was a little hard-nosed and a little too focused and he rubbed people up the wrong way, but in time he'd learn the skills needed to be a well-rounded businessman. Maggie hadn't seen any of that drive in Joshua and had no idea what to make of him.

The matter wasn't settled, not by a long shot, but for the moment it had to be forgotten because a truck was approaching, and it sounded like Frank's. The last thing he needed was something to mar the first gathering of his entire family in weeks. She addressed Julian. "If it's as you said, then fine. It'd upset your father greatly to hear you weren't getting along."

Neither brother replied.

She nodded to them both and returned to the kitchen to help Janella set out the meal, under no illusion that she'd achieved anything.

CHAPTER 3

*J*oshua sighed with relief. The truck wasn't Dad's. One of the hands had stopped to give an update on a new foal. The timing of the birth had been fortunate since their vet was leaving. After more than twenty years on the cattle station, Simon and his wife, Sara, were relocating to the seaside town of Broome. A lifelong dream finally realised.

If only Joshua could do the same.

But he walked a fine line. Every day, a deep longing to leave the station filled him, consumed him, but each day, rational, sensible reasons why he should stay kept him there. A battle waged inside him, and each morning he wondered which side would win. Today, he would stay. But tomorrow? He wasn't sure.

Maggie's entrance may have stopped the argument between him and Julian, but only for a time. Eventually it would continue as it always did. Julian would never understand him, and Joshua had almost given up trying to explain himself to his older brother. He was a man, not a child, and capable of making decisions for himself. He was tired of Julian telling him what to do. *Who did he think he was?* And Maggie. What right did she have to interfere?

Words his mother would hate to hear spewed from his mouth. Clenching his teeth, he kicked the red dirt with his boots. With Julian inside raring for another argument, and Maggie ready to pounce, there was no way he'd go back inside until everyone else had arrived for lunch.

But he needed to compose himself before Dad arrived. Not much got past his father. He had a knack of knowing when something was wrong, but until now, Joshua had been able to hide his discontent from him. Or at least he thought he had.

His hand moved to the phone in his pocket without thinking. Pulling it out, he stared at it. It was pointless calling. She never answered. She didn't want to talk to him. He wasn't sure what he'd done to upset her, but she didn't even message back these days.

He shoved the phone back into his pocket as Sean arrived in his truck.

His cousin jumped out, a cloud of red dust billowing in the air as he landed on the ground. "Hey, cuz. What are you doin' out here? Thought you'd be inside eatin' lunch."

"I needed some fresh air," Joshua replied.

Sean's gaze shifted between the house and Joshua. "Julian's inside, isn't he?"

Joshua leaned against the truck and nodded. "Yep, he's in there, alright."

"Figured as much. He's the only one who could chase you out of your own home."

Joshua nodded. It was true.

Sean draped an arm around his shoulders. "Don't look so glum, cuz. Your brother's full of hot air. As much as he barks, his bite's nothin'. Let's go inside and eat. The sooner we get done, the sooner we can leave."

Joshua raked a hand across his dark hair and drew a deep breath. His cousin knew exactly what to say to make him feel better. He made life on the station bearable, but like Joshua, Sean wanted to leave and find his way in the world. He only stayed because of Joshua. "Okay. Let's go," Joshua said, sighing heavily.

As they walked up the steps and approached the door, Nathan and Olivia came from the other direction along the verandah. His sister smiled, while Nathan gave a curt nod. Joshua and his brother-in-law didn't exactly see eye-to-eye. They had no open quarrel as Joshua had with Julian, but he was sure Nathan still held a grudge against him for not stepping up to help the family after Joshua and Olivia's mum died. Nathan and Olivia had willingly given up their jobs and their comfortable life in Darwin to help out on the station and had been there ever since. Joshua, on the other hand, had escaped to the rodeo circuit. It had been his way of coping with his mother's death. Not that he'd admit that to anyone.

There wasn't anything obvious. It was simply a feeling. An underlying resentment. But Joshua didn't care. It was just another reason why he wanted to leave.

Once inside, his sister made a beeline for the kitchen while Nathan walked with Joshua and Sean to the dining room, but he headed straight for Julian who stood by the window staring out. By the rigidness in his body, Joshua could tell Julian was still geed up over their argument. Joshua cast him a narrowed glare and then stood with Sean at the other end of the room. The further away from his brother and brother-in-law he was, the better.

They hadn't always been at each other's throats. There was a time when he, Julian and Olivia had been happy. When they were children. Before their mother died.

"Another screwup."

The words stung Joshua's ears from across the room. His gaze shot to where Julian stood with Nathan. As he met his brother's steely gaze, his jaw clenched.

"What's he talking about?" Sean nudged him.

"Nothing," Joshua replied.

"He's trying to blame you for something, isn't he? He's always trying to blame you for something."

"Quiet."

"No," Sean continued, huffing. The vein in his head pulsed. Before Joshua could stop him, Sean left his side and barrelled across the room.

He fronted Julian, his chest out. "What are you blaming Josh for now?"

"What does it matter to you, Sean?" Julian's tone was sharp as he glanced in Joshua's direction. He was obviously itching to continue the argument from earlier, and Sean was only making it worse.

Joshua rushed after him. He had to separate them.

Sean stepped closer. "Why are you always blaming Joshua for something?"

33

Julian scoffed. "Blame can't be laid if there's none to be had."

Joshua's jaw clenched as he tried to restrain his growing anger. "What does that mean?"

Julian turned in his direction. "It means, when you're irresponsible, there's always something to mess up, something others have to fix."

"Someone like you?" Sean snapped. "As if you could do half of what *we* do. I don't see you taking stuck up city slickers on overnight cattle drives. Handling the livestock. You know, actual *work*. You just sit around looking at numbers and give orders as if you're a king."

Julian's chest heaved as he decreased the gap between them. "Are you questioning my work ethic? You think because I'm not out there rounding up cattle I'm not working? I work ten times harder than you. Do you have any idea what it takes to run this station? No, you don't. You just sit on a horse and chase women."

Joshua seethed. How dare Julian downplay what he and Sean did. Every day they did stuff his brother would never lower himself to do. He approached Julian and shoved him in the chest, pushing him back. "You have some nerve, you know that? What gives you the right to talk about what we do like that? What we do is just as important as what you do. If not more so. We're keeping this place afloat."

THE SOUND of angry voices drifted into the kitchen from the dining room. The three women looked at each other.

"They can't be at it again." Janella sighed heavily.

"It certainly sounds that way," Maggie said, defeat in her voice. Her efforts at mediation had achieved nothing.

Janella shook her head as she grabbed some mitts and pulled a dish from the oven.

Olivia dropped the dishtowel on the counter. "I've had enough of this. Dad will be here any second and the two of them are acting like children."

"Don't get caught in the middle," Janella cautioned.

"Why not? They're my brothers and they sound like immature kids. You'd think by now they would have settled their differences. They can't keep doing this. It's ridiculous." Folding her arms, Olivia leaned back against the counter.

Until today, Maggie hadn't seen this side of the Goddard family. Although it saddened her that the brothers weren't getting along, that they'd behave in such a manner knowing she would hear them suggested that they accepted her as part of the family, and that knowledge made her want to help even more.

The voices rose in intensity.

She dared to delve deeper. "What's it all about? It can't be something that just happened today, surely."

Olivia sighed. "No, but they're at it pretty much every day. Julian and Joshua are like chalk and cheese, but since Mum died, they're like two grown babies arguing about who's right, and neither wants to budge. I've just about had enough of it. I have half a mind to tell Dad everything. He won't allow it to go on."

Maggie nodded. Olivia was right. Frank would never allow his offspring to behave in such a manner. He'd get to the bottom of whatever it was and make things right. But the wounds seemed longstanding. Surely Frank was aware of the feud. But she couldn't imagine he'd allow it to continue if he did. "Have either of you discussed it with him?"

Olivia exhaled deeply. "No. He had enough worry when the station was in trouble, and now he seems so content. Despite what I said, I wouldn't want to tell him. I'd just like Joshua and Julian to grow up. But I think the only person who can help them is Dad."

Maggie shook her head. "There's someone else."

"Who?" Olivia's brows scrunched.

"Well, people can only do so much, but God can change hearts. I think that's what your brothers need."

"You're right, but they also need a good tanning," Olivia replied with a chuckle.

"I'd love to see that." Janella laughed. "Can you imagine Julian over someone's knee?"

Despite the argument in the next room, the mood in the kitchen had lightened and Maggie was glad. "That *would* be a sight," she agreed. "But I think we should try to calm them before Frank gets here, especially if we want to keep this from him a little longer. Maybe we can devise a plan to help Joshua and Julian understand each other better. If we can, then Frank won't have to be involved."

"I'm willing to try," Janella said.

"Me too," Olivia added. "Though I warn you, the Goddard men can be as stubborn as mules at times, especially Julian."

"Hey now! That's my husband you're talking about. He isn't as bad as all that. He's gotten better." Janella's gaze swung from Olivia to Maggie. "He has."

36

Olivia took the dish from Janella. "Yes, he has, but he's still Julian. He likes being right, Janella. He always has, even when it's obvious he's wrong. I'm simply warning Maggie. If she wants to help, she needs to know what she's facing. I've known these boys their entire lives and I know what they're like."

Janella nodded. "Okay. But right now, we'd better get this food on the table before they eat each other."

"They've stopped." Maggie angled her head towards the dining room.

Janella and Olivia looked at each other, their brows lifting.

Maggie wasn't sure when the argument had ceased, nor what had caused it to stop, but she couldn't have been more relieved since Frank would be there any minute.

CHAPTER 4

$\mathcal{F}$rank had been eagerly anticipating the midday meeting with his family. A week earlier, he'd received a call from Ravi Tamala, the Indonesian businessman who'd helped turn around the fortunes of Goddard Downs by contracting to buy a large proportion of their processed beef. Now he was offering an even better deal. He was expanding his business and needed more product, and he wanted to give Goddard Downs the first chance to supply it.

If they agreed, it would mean adjusting their existing contract and increasing the demand on the cattle station's stock by a quarter. It was a big deal that could be lucrative, but it would also place more pressure on their resources, especially with Simon, their livestock vet, retiring.

That morning, Frank had studied the numbers for about the tenth time. Ravi had sent the details of the proposed contract, and Frank liked what he saw. The cattle drives were doing well and had supplemented the station's primary income, but Goddard Downs was a cattle station, not a tourist destination. Returning the focus to cattle production would please him no end.

But would the rest of the family agree? He wasn't sure. And having handed the reins to Julian, Frank didn't hold as much weight as he once had. But still, he hoped they'd be excited about the proposal and would at least be prepared to discuss it, although Julian would be annoyed that Ravi continued to liaise with Frank, and not him. It was simply because they connected, something Julian hadn't yet been able to achieve, although Frank hoped that in time his eldest son would develop his people skills.

He finished his coffee, closed his computer and headed outside. His step was light as he whistled and climbed into his truck, a smile creeping into his face as his gaze landed on the new garden bed Maggie had recently planted outside their cabin. Already the shrubs were sprouting new growth and the colourful annuals were in full bloom, making the garden bright and cheery. She had such a green thumb. In fact, everything about her made him smile. Marrying her was the best thing he'd done.

He cranked the engine and the truck roared to life and he headed to the workshop to pick up Caleb, his eldest grandson, to take him to lunch. Caleb was working on a motorbike engine with one of the hands, and even at his young age, he displayed good understanding and interest in all things mechanical. Frank wanted to encourage that interest and was pleased that Julian didn't mind and Janella approved. Caleb would be leaving for boarding school before they knew it, and Frank wanted to ensure he left with good memories.

Stopping the car outside the workshop, Frank honked the horn to get his grandson's attention.

A few minutes later, Caleb, tall and gangly, appeared with grease on his shirt and a grin on his face. He ran around to the passenger side and climbed in. "Hi, Grandpa."

"Hi, there Caleb. How's the engine coming along?" Frank asked, engaging first gear.

"Great! Tom said it needs a full overhaul and he's happy for me to help him with it."

Caleb's enthusiasm warmed Frank's heart. It seemed such a long time since the sullen veneer had dropped from his grandson's face and a more cheerful, content boy had emerged. He thanked God every day for Caleb's transformation. It had been such a blessing to introduce him to the Lord, and since that day, Caleb's appetite for the Word had grown rapidly and they'd shared many special moments discussing passages of scripture and praying together. Frank would sorely miss those times once Caleb left for school.

They continued chatting about the plans for the motorbike until Frank stopped the truck in front of the homestead. After climbing out, they walked up the steps together, Frank's hand resting lightly on Caleb's shoulder, but as they approached the door, sounds of raised voices drifting down the hallway stopped him in his tracks.

"You'd better go and find your mother," Frank said to his grandson.

Frank winced at the puzzled expression on Caleb's face. Why did his grown sons have to behave so immaturely? "Sorry, son, but I need to sort this out."

Caleb nodded, and on Frank's direction, headed around the verandah to avoid going through the house.

With Caleb out of the way, Frank drew a deep breath and strode down the hall to the dining room.

All four men in the room turned and faced him.

"What's going on here?" Frank demanded as his gaze narrowed and landed on his sons who stared at him with open mouths.

"I asked a question. What's going on? I could hear the two of you from outside."

The expression on his sons' faces reminded him of when they were children and they'd gotten caught doing something they shouldn't. They wore the same sheepish looks now.

"Which one of you is going to tell me?" Frank insisted, levelling an earnest gaze at Julian and then Joshua. He didn't care who spoke first so long as he got the truth. Whatever the problem was, he was sure it could be remedied, but with his sons, an intermediary seemed to always be a necessity. He folded his arms and waited to see who'd be the first to talk.

DUST BILLOWED in the rear-view mirror as Stella drove towards Goddard Downs. The midday sun streaming in through the windscreen was warm on her skin, and the wind whipped her hair as she gripped the steering wheel to keep the Jeep steady as it bounced over the corrugations in the road. Her heart pounded as she uttered a silent prayer for strength and courage. This was her last chance. If Frank Goddard turned her down, there was no Plan B. That was it. She was finished. Her family's cattle station would be lost forever. She pressed her foot down harder on the pedal.

Ask and it will be given to you; seek and you will find; knock and the door will be opened to you. For everyone who asks receives; the one who seeks finds; and to the one who knocks, the door will be opened. The words echoed in her head as clear as if her grandmother was beside her reading them. The words offered Stella hope. If she believed, and she sought, she would find all the answers she was looking for. Even if it meant knocking on the door of Goddard Downs.

The expansive cattle station was much larger than her family's modest one, but that was inconsequential. She didn't care that her workload might be doubled, or even tripled, so long as she could save her family's station. That was all that mattered. But first, she had to prove to the bank that she could afford the mortgage on the property, and that meant securing a job and earning an income. Her parents had completely given up on the idea and weren't going to help. Their defeat, and their decision to leave it all behind and move south, was heartbreaking, but Stella couldn't let their actions stop her. She still believed she could save the property, and as long as she believed, she wouldn't give up.

After turning off the main road, she made her way along the rutted dusty road that led to the Goddard Downs homestead. The track crossed several creeks which were almost dry but would quickly become impassable when the rains hit.

After another thirty minutes, she spotted the sprawling ranch-style home up ahead. There didn't appear to be any designated parking area, so she parked her Jeep some distance from the house in the shade of a large gum tree. No one seemed to be around, but since it was lunchtime, she assumed they'd be inside.

Her hands felt clammy, and not just because of the heat. Her future, and that of Indigo Downs, depended on the outcome of her unscheduled meeting with Frank Goddard. Perhaps she should have called and enquired about the job rather than simply turning up, but she knew it would be more difficult to refuse her offer face to face. And she knew how to lay on the charm when she had to. If only it hadn't worked so well with Joshua. She liked the younger Goddard son, but he was a loose cannon, and he was persistent. Her phone had beeped with another missed call message from him as she came back into range only a few moments ago. She wouldn't call him now since she would no doubt see him shortly. He'd be surprised to see her after all this time, especially since she'd been avoiding his calls. But she wasn't here to revive their fleeting relationship. She was here to get a job.

She quickly checked her appearance in the mirror. She wore little makeup. It was pointless in this heat since it slid off within moments of application, but she did apply some light pink lip-gloss and smoothed her hair.

As her gaze shifted to the homestead, her heart raced. She began to recite the speech she'd rehearsed a thousand times. There were a zillion reasons why she would be a great replacement for their vet, and she'd decided she'd use them all if doing so would get her the job. But the confidence she'd felt earlier had slipped away and been replaced with doubt. What had made her think she'd be good enough for the position? It was a mistake to come. But no, she couldn't think like that. She wouldn't fail. She couldn't.

Unable to stem the tide of anxious thoughts that besieged her, she bowed her head and prayed. *Heavenly Father, there is none before You and none like You. You are Jehovah Jireh, the great Provider, and Lord, how I need Your provision now. I can't do this alone. You know I've done all I can, but now I ask You to do all You can on my behalf. Every other door has closed, and this is the only one left.*

I don't understand Your ways, and why of all places You'd bring me here, but I trust You. I know You'd never lead me where You couldn't sustain me. I know You only desire my good and that Your plans for me are already established. I ask that You give me the grace to walk into this house and speak the words that will get me the job. I need Your help, Lord. There is no one else. You're my only hope. Show Yourself faithful, Lord. In Jesus' precious name. Amen.

Her heart no longer raced, though the beat was still strong and clear in her ears as she stepped down from her Jeep and closed the door behind her. She smoothed the wrinkles in her khaki shirt and shorts as she strode towards the house. She'd chosen to wear practical attire instead of a more feminine skirt or dress since her task was to convince Frank Goddard she could be his head vet, and she doubted a dress or skirt would help her achieve that goal.

The door seemed imposing as she approached, but she kept her head high and tried to remember to breathe as she reached it, raised her hand, and prepared to knock.

The last thing she expected was for the door to fly open and a flustered Joshua Goddard barrel through it, almost crashing into her.

"Joshua?"

His eyes widened. "Stella?"

CHAPTER 5

*T*he sight before him was not expected. Today was supposed to be a good day, an opportunity for his family to come together under one roof for the first time in weeks. Yet, here they were, bickering.

Frank couldn't help the disappointment in his heart as he momentarily gazed around the room, noting the photos that went back three generations. There was one photo, taken when his children were still young, and Esther was with them. They'd been smiling then. A toddler, Joshua, was on Julian's lap while Esther held Olivia, and Frank's arms were wrapped around her shoulders. He remembered that day. They were no arguments then.

"What's going on here?" He repeated the question.

"I'll tell you." Sean stepped forward, anger etched into the contours of his face as he began to explain. "Julian's throwing his weight around and blaming stuff on Joshua unfairly."

"I did no such thing." Julian's eyes narrowed.

"Quiet," Frank said firmly. "You had your chance and you didn't take it. Let Sean speak, then, I'll hear you."

Frank didn't miss the gratified grin that spread across his nephew's face or the fact that Joshua remained silent. "Explain what you mean, Sean."

"Julian is constantly looking for something to blame Joshua for, when he's done nothing wrong. If it's not one thing, it's another. How he speaks to female guests, or the fact that we're friendly with them. Just because Julian doesn't know how to have a good time doesn't mean that Joshua and I don't."

"I know very well how 'good' a time you're having and that's not the type of image we want to portray," Julian interrupted once more.

"Julian, give your cousin a chance to finish what he's saying. I'd like to hear it."

Julian's eyes widened. "Are you really going to listen to this?"

Frank took a deep breath. "Yes, Julian, I am. Your cousin deserves the same courtesy and respect as anyone else. I'd hear any of you out. I'd appreciate it if you'd do the same and allow me to understand what's going on here."

Julian had held his tongue after that, but Frank could see it was with difficulty. Julian never had an issue with speaking his mind and ensuring he was heard. Neither did Sean. It was Joshua who seemed to shy away from speaking, more now than when his mother was alive. He was allowing Sean to speak, but it was Joshua he really wanted to hear from.

Sean continued his speech, outlining the tyrant he believed Julian to be and how he constantly sought to defame Joshua at every turn. Frank regarded his youngest son, who stood silently, as if the conversation had nothing to do with him.

"Joshua, do you have anything to add?" he questioned, hoping his son would speak up and be honest.

Joshua levelled a placid look in his direction. "No."

"Come on, Josh. Tell him what Julian's been doing," Sean protested.

Joshua remained silent as the sound of shuffling feet caught Frank's attention. It was Maggie, Olivia and Janella coming in from the kitchen, the lunch dishes in their hands and curious expressions on their faces. Maggie's fell, but Frank had only a moment to note her change in countenance before he noticed Joshua heading for the door.

"Where are you going?" Frank called after him.

"I'm suddenly not hungry," Joshua replied as he continued on his path.

He couldn't leave. To Frank, it seemed that all he saw of his younger son was his back and he was tired of it. He wanted them to be close. He wanted to understand him. Frank followed him to the front door, determined that this time, he wouldn't escape. "Don't go, Josh. Can't we talk about it?"

"Talk about what, Dad?" Joshua replied, turning to face him. "There's nothing to talk about. Julian will explain everything. He always does."

His words cut. "Yes, he does. It doesn't change the fact that I still want to hear from you. I want to hear your side," Frank continued. His tone was gentle, almost pleading. He wanted his son to come back, not just to the room, but also to his life. Joshua was always trying to escape, and that broke Frank's heart. He wanted to have back the boy he'd bounced on his

47

knee and who'd stood by his side watching him work, wanting to know everything he did. He wanted them to be a real family, the way they used to be. Before Esther died. She'd be heartbroken to see the way her boys were behaving.

"It doesn't matter, Dad. It hasn't mattered for a long time." Despondency tainted Joshua's words and further tore at Frank's heart.

"It does," he replied. "It does to me."

"Not to me," Joshua answered as he turned the handle.

The last thing Frank expected to hear was a female voice on the other side of the door.

Stepping closer, Frank peered around Joshua. A pretty blonde stood in the doorway. Her face was vaguely familiar, but he couldn't immediately place her. Her gaze was firmly fixed on Joshua until she noticed Frank standing behind him.

"Mr. Goddard," she said, her expression quickly changing to a smile.

"Miss?" Frank's forehead creased as he stepped around Joshua.

"Martin. Stella Martin. I'm sorry to stop by unannounced, but I wanted to speak to you. Do you have some time?"

The name rang a bell. Martin. Of course. The Martins owned a smaller cattle station closer to town and had once been guests at one of their past get togethers.

"Actually, we were just sitting down to lunch and we have some important matters to discuss. Could you come back another time?"

"I can wait," she replied, her expression determined.

Frank's brow furrowed. "What's this about?"

"Your station."

Joshua still stood between them. He looked torn, as if unsure whether to leave or stay. Frank wondered at the sudden change when a moment before he seemed set on leaving. He was sure the young woman's statement had something to do with it. If she wanted to see him about the station, then he'd listen to her. Perhaps it was also a way to keep Joshua there.

"Josh, would you tell Maggie to start the meal without me. I'll join you after I've spoken to Miss Martin."

Joshua looked at his father, and then at Stella, before turning and walking quietly back into the house.

Frank breathed a sigh of a relief as his son disappeared down the hallway, leaving him alone with Stella. "Please, follow me."

They walked to the office and he offered Stella a seat before lowering himself into the chair behind the desk. She had a large brown envelope in her hand. He leaned forward. "Now, tell me. What can I do for you?"

She folded her hands in her lap and fixed her gaze on his. "I've come to offer you my services."

"Don't you work for your parents?"

She nodded. "I did, but they've closed the station and moved to Cootamundra. I'm the only one left."

The news took him by surprise, but as he saw the pained look in her eyes, he understood. Many of the local cattle stations had suffered greatly after the live cattle ban had been imposed. "I'm sorry to hear that," he said, meaning it.

"Thank you. The ban caused a lot of a trouble for us. We couldn't pull ourselves out, but I'm hoping to change that."

"Change it? How?"

"That's why I wanted to speak to you. I heard that your

large animal vet is leaving. I have all the necessary credentials, plus years of experience. I know your herd's larger than Indigo's, but I can handle it. If I have a job, I can buy Indigo back."

The look in her eyes spoke to Frank. It was a look he recognised. It was the steely determination that had been in his own eyes every day as he'd tried to figure out how to save Goddard Downs. "You want to get Indigo back?" he asked.

Her chin lifted. "Yes. It's my home."

Frank understood how she felt, but the task was formidable, as was the job. He clasped his hands on his desk and leaned forward. "Are you sure you know what you'd be getting yourself into?"

"I do," she said with a nod.

Without question, they needed a new vet. It was one of the topics for discussion at the meeting, but they hadn't started searching yet. Now, here was Stella, offering to fill a post they hadn't advertised. It puzzled him slightly as to how she knew about it, although he knew that word spread quickly amidst the cattle station hands. Someone must have said something.

He regarded her thoughtfully as he tapped the desk with his thumb. She needed a job, and they needed a vet. Was this of God? It seemed too coincidental not to be. But still, he couldn't just hire her. Since he'd given Julian responsibility, the decision had to predominately be his, although they'd all have input. "Do you have a resumé?"

Reaching into the envelope on her lap, she removed the document and handed it to him across the desk.

Frank glanced over it. It was a very commendable record of her education and experience. He was impressed.

"What do you think?"

He looked at her. There was tenacity in her eyes. The same tenacity that he remembered in his mother's eyes when she was younger. This young woman needed help and wasn't afraid to ask for it.

"I can see that you're capable," Frank replied. "However, the decision to hire you isn't mine alone. I'll have to discuss it with my eldest son and the rest of the family before a decision is made."

Stella nodded silently, disappointment on her face. Though he wished he could hire her on the spot, he simply couldn't.

"I understand," she said quietly.

Frank gave her an encouraging smile. "Stella? May I call you Stella?"

"Of course."

"I promise I won't make you wait long. As soon as I've had a chance to discuss this with my family, I'll be in contact." He pushed his chair back and stood.

"That's fair," Stella replied, gathering her things before she stood.

Frank held out his hand. "It was nice seeing you again, Stella. I'm sorry it had to be under such circumstances."

She took his hand and shook it. "Thank you, Mr. Goddard. I feel the same."

"Let me walk you out."

He walked her to the door. It was a silent journey and Frank couldn't help but think of the fortuitousness of her arrival. He saw her out and waited until she got into her Jeep before closing the door. He took a deep breath and headed down the hallway to join his family.

CHAPTER 6

*M*aggie had stood silently while Frank went
after Joshua and prayed he would have the
right words to make him come back.

Her silent prayer had been answered minutes later when
Joshua trudged back into the room and informed her that his
father would be along soon but to start without him. She told
the others, but when Frank and a young woman walked along
the verandah together, the interest of all was piqued.

She had no idea where the young woman had come from
nor who she was, but Maggie didn't miss Joshua staring after
her as she walked with his father.

Call it maternal intuition, but Maggie was sure the two
knew each other.

"Who is she?" Olivia asked as she settled Isobel on her lap.

"I don't know," Maggie replied, taking her seat. She turned
to Joshua. "Do you know who she is?"

Joshua barely looked in Maggie's direction as he answered. "Stella Martin."

"Martin? As in the Martins of Indigo Downs?" Julian barked.

"Yes." Joshua's reply was short but civil. He took his seat beside Sean, who whispered in his ear as he sat. Their tense expressions intrigued Maggie.

"What does she want?" Julian continued.

"I don't know," Joshua replied.

Julian remained standing as everyone settled in their seats. "Maybe I should see what's going on."

"Your father said to carry on. I'm sure he would have asked for you if he needed you," Maggie said.

Julian pursed his lips. She got the feeling he didn't like her involvement, but she was sure Frank wouldn't want him bursting in if it was a private matter.

"Why don't you say grace?" She gave a smile she hoped would placate him.

"Sure." He bowed his head and gave thanks before he took his seat.

They all ate in relative silence as they waited for Frank to return. Questions loomed in the air about Miss Martin's sudden arrival, but also regarding the argument between Julian and Joshua. How would Frank take it? What would he do? What did Miss Martin want?

Maggie sat on the other side of Joshua and noticed he kept looking in the direction where Frank and the young woman had disappeared. He looked uncomfortable, and if she had to guess, she was sure he would have preferred being anywhere else. Perhaps she could ease that discomfort.

"How was everything this morning, Joshua?" she asked, trying to break the icy chill that hovered over the room.

Joshua lifted his head. "Fine."

"That's good. I imagine the cattle drives can be exhausting. I admire the hard work you and Sean put in."

Sean blinked as a smirk grew on his face. "At least someone around here recognises how hard we work." He glanced at Julian.

"Quiet, Sean," Joshua said in a low, barely audible voice. He met Maggie's gaze and gave a small smile. "Thank you."

Maggie gave a nod and studied him as he toyed with his food. "Do you know Miss Martin well?" she finally asked.

Her question caused an instant reaction. Joshua's gaze shot up and he wore an almost guilty expression. "No. Not well."

Maggie knew he wasn't telling the truth but didn't press the issue. Whatever connection there was between him and Stella Martin, it was obvious he didn't want to talk about it. What was clear, however, was that whatever troubled him was significant as he pushed his food from one part of his plate to the other, barely taking a bite. Maggie knew a troubled soul when she saw one.

Lord, please help Joshua. Whatever's bothering him, let him know he's loved and that he can turn to You.

The entire family stiffened as a door closed and footsteps sounded on the verandah. Maggie glimpsed Frank as he and Stella passed by. Minutes later, he entered the room and took his place at the table by Maggie's side. "Sorry for being late. I had an unexpected, but timely visitor."

"What did she want?" Julian asked immediately.

"A job," Frank replied.

"A job? Why would she be looking for a job here?" Julian's forehead creased. "She's got her own station to work on."

"Her family's lost it and she's looking for work." Frank placed an envelope on the table. "After lunch, we can review her résumé and discuss the matter. Right now, I'm famished."

Maggie glanced in Joshua's direction. His expression was neutral, but Sean leaned in and whispered something in his ear and Joshua whispered back. Their behaviour was piquing Maggie's curiosity more and more.

Frank cleared his throat. "Joshua and Julian, after lunch I'd like to continue the conversation I started with you."

"I can't." Joshua spoke firmly. "There are things to get ready for the guests arriving this afternoon. Besides, it wasn't important."

"I think it is," Frank insisted.

"Forget about it, Dad. It was nothing," Julian piped up. "Just a brotherly disagreement."

"That's what concerns me," Frank stated. "There seems to be more disagreement than agreement of late, and I want to know why."

Neither Julian nor Joshua answered. Maggie looked from one to the other. She reached for Frank's hand and squeezed it. Whatever was happening in the family, she wanted him to know he had her support. She would be beside him just as he was beside her. Whatever help she could give, she would. Julian and Joshua were her family, now, whether they liked it or not.

WITH THE MEETING FINALLY OVER, Joshua couldn't wait to get out of the house. Having Stella turn up at Goddard Downs had thrown him completely, and the possibility of her working on the station as their vet was totally unexpected. No words had been spoken between them. It was like she hadn't wanted to acknowledge they knew each other, but that was confusing. The last time they'd seen each other in Alice Springs she'd promised to stay in touch. She wasn't loose like a lot of the girls on the rodeo circuit who seemed to only be there for the cowboys. In fact, she'd been employed as one of the vets, and while Sean was boozing and womanising, he and Stella had simply spent time together, talking, laughing, and dancing. Although they'd not progressed further than friendship, she'd managed to weave her way around his heart and successfully melt it. Not that he'd given her any indication of his feelings. As far as she was concerned, they were just good friends.

But he'd never met a girl like her. Not that he'd met many living on the station, and most of the girls on the circuit left him cold. Stella had morals, and she was clever, not to mention, drop-dead gorgeous.

He could still remember what she was wearing the last night he saw her. She'd pretty much taken his breath away when she showed up for dinner in a crisp white button-up shirt, sleeves rolled to the elbows, skinny jeans, and high-heeled boots. Her hair was down and smelled like something floral. It was all he could do to keep his eyes off her. Following dinner, they'd boogied together all night. It was the most fun he'd had, ever. But then she left to return home. Her grandmother had fallen ill, and since they were close, she left straight away.

Joshua didn't know why she hadn't returned his calls or messages. In the one brief message she'd sent, she'd told him she had a lot of stuff going on, and that maybe one day they could catch up. That had been it, until today, when she turned up out of the blue looking for a job. *Why hadn't she told him she was coming?* Did she have no idea what impact her turning up like that would have on him? *Women.* He could do without them, thank-you very much.

"Come on, Seano. Let's get this gear packed." Sean hadn't been involved in the meeting and had been sitting outside waiting for him. Joshua jumped into the driver's seat of the truck they used for transporting the cattle drive gear from the big shed near the homestead to the stables where the tourists assembled. Sean climbed into the passenger seat, and for once, remained silent.

Joshua cranked the engine, huffed out a huge breath, and spun the wheels in the gravel as he hit the pedal a bit too hard.

"That bad, huh?" Sean asked, raising a brow.

"I don't want to talk about it."

"Righteo."

Joshua needed to calm down. Adrenalin coursed through his veins after the meeting, during which his pompous brother had continued their argument, albeit subtly, but Julian had gotten in enough barbs and comments to niggle Joshua, even if the others hadn't noticed. He shouldn't react the way he did, but his brother had a knack of pushing his buttons. He thumped the steering wheel and blew out another huge breath. "Sorry, mate. Julian got to me again."

"He's a bully, that's all I can say."

Joshua was loath to agree out loud. Julian was his brother, after all, but Sean was right. Julian was a bully. Pity no one else saw it.

"You should be running the place, not him."

"No chance of that happening. I was never a contender, and I never will be. Not while Julian and Olivia are here. Julian's the star and Olivia has the brains. All I have is brawn."

Sean chuckled. "You really are in a bad way."

"I've made up my mind. As soon as they find someone to replace us, we're out of here."

Sean straightened, his expression brightening. "No way!"

"Yep. I've had enough."

"Cool, dude. I thought I'd never hear you say it. But what about that chick? What was she doin' here?"

"Looking for a job."

"Really. Wouldn't you want to stay?"

"Nope. She's too stuck up."

"That's what I thought. Think of all the chicks we'll be able to hook up with after we leave here."

"Yeah…" But as red dust billowed behind the truck as he steered it towards the shed, his mother's voice echoed inside his head… *The heart is deceitful above all things and beyond cure. Who can understand it? "I, the Lord search the heart and examine the mind, to reward each person according to their conduct, according to what their deeds deserve."*

No. He wouldn't listen. For as long as he could remember, Joshua had dutifully performed all that was required and expected of him, but to what avail? No more. He was done with trying to please. They could stick the job and the station.

And God could mind His own business. After this drive, Joshua and Sean would be out of here, replacements found or not.

A<small>FTER LEAVING</small> G<small>ODDARD</small> D<small>OWNS</small>, Stella was reluctant to immediately return to the apartment she was sharing in town with her cousin, Elizabeth. She felt deflated. She'd been so sure she'd be offered the job on the spot, but now, walking away with empty hands and only a promise of a phone call, the spark of hope she'd held on the way there was now extinguished.

Had she really expected the position to be offered to her after one short meeting? Perhaps her expectation had been unreasonable. But she'd been so sure that God would answer her prayers. Why hadn't He?

Instead of heading straight back to town, she decided to detour via the Purnululu National Park. She was in no hurry to return to the apartment and Elizabeth's questions for which she had no answers.

Three hours later, Stella reached the park, climbed out of the Jeep and stretched. It had been a long drive as she battled with her emotions, and a walk amongst the orange and black striped sandstone domes of the Bungle Bungle Range would do her good. Taking a small backpack from the back seat, she locked the car and headed down the pathway, gazing at the giant beehive-like domes etched with horizontal lines as if the earth had marked them as a way of tracking their age.

How could people see such majesty and not believe in God?

His craftsmanship was everywhere for those willing to take the time to see it. And she had more than enough time now the station was closed and she was jobless.

Every time she thought of its loss, pain tore at her insides. Her parents had worked so hard for so long. It didn't seem fair that they should lose their home. Their livelihood. She should have done more. If only they'd told her how bad it was sooner, she might have been able to do something to save it. But now, they'd given up and walked away.

She had to get it back. Indigo was their home. How could her parents leave without a fight?

A sigh rose from deep inside her as she trudged on. There was no guarantee of securing the job at Goddard Downs. What if she was forced to accept that Indigo was lost forever? What then? What would she do? Where would she go? She could only sleep in Elizabeth's guest room for so long.

Time rolled on as she wandered between the domes. So lost in her thoughts, she hadn't noticed the storm clouds on the horizon until she returned to her car. Not that anything would come of them since the start of the rainy season was still weeks away. But still, the day was quickly drawing to a close and darkness would soon engulf the land. And Elizabeth would be worried about her.

Stella turned the key in the ignition and headed for town.

Arriving well into the evening, she parked her car in the designated parking space, and as she approached the door, did her best to put on a positive attitude. She'd done all she could —the rest was up to God. She'd pled her case to Frank Goddard, and she was sure he understood her plight. But what if he couldn't convince his family to employ her? No, she wouldn't entertain that thought. Going to Goddard Downs hadn't been her idea. It had to be of God. He hadn't led her there if He didn't intend for her to get the job. She simply had to be patient.

Those thoughts filled her unsettled mind and anxious heart as she put the key into the lock and quietly opened the door. There was something else to consider. What if she did get the job? Then she'd be forced to see Joshua every day. She wasn't sure she was prepared for that, but she had time to figure it out. The most important thing was landing the position.

Stella was barely in the door before Elizabeth, petite and dark-haired with olive skin and a round face, bounded up to her waving her phone. "Where've you been? I've been worried sick. I was about to call the police."

"I'm sorry. I took a drive and lost track of time."

"Lost track of time? Where did you go? You were supposed to go to Goddard Downs and come back to tell me about it."

"I detoured via the Bungle Bungles," Stella answered, setting her backpack on the floor. "You know how I am when I'm there."

Elizabeth frowned. "I know, but it doesn't mean you can just disappear. Why didn't you answer your phone?"

Stella took her phone from her pocket. The screen was black. "It must have died. I didn't even notice."

Elizabeth slapped her arm. "You're supposed to charge your phone when you're going such distances."

"I know. I'm sorry. I guess I was nervous about Goddard Downs and forgot." Stella stepped past her and flopped down on the nearest cushioned chair.

Elizabeth sat on the couch across from her. "So, what happened?"

Stella shrugged. "Nothing."

"You didn't get it?"

"I don't know yet. I spoke with Frank Goddard and I think it went well, but he said he had to discuss it with his family and he'll let me know." Stella closed her eyes and covered them with her arm. All of a sudden, she felt tired, as if all the stresses of the past weeks were finally catching up with her.

"You'll get it," Elizabeth said confidently.

Stella peeked at her from beneath her arm. "How can you be so sure?"

"Because, whatever it is the Lord has for you, it's at Goddard Downs. Why else would every other avenue have failed, if not to guide you there? I told you from the second you heard about that job that it was for you, but you had your reasons for avoiding that place." Elizabeth looked at her keenly. "Did you see Joshua?"

At the mention of his name, Stella's heart quickened. She swallowed hard and tried to sound casual. "Yes."

"What happened?"

"Nothing. He opened the door. That's it."

"That's it? You didn't talk at all?"

"No. What would we have to talk about?" Stella straightened. She couldn't tell Elizabeth that the second she saw Joshua her heart had leapt. It would only convince her that her ideas about Stella and Joshua were correct. Elizabeth believed he was the perfect match for her, but Stella didn't share the sentiment.

"I don't get it. You talked about him for months after

meeting him and then you just stopped. Now, you have the chance to see him and you say nothing happened?" Doubt laced Elizabeth's words, but Stella was telling the truth.

"Nothing happened. The time we spent together, however brief and ill-advised, is over. Let it go, Liz. Joshua and I are in very different places in life. We should give each other as much room as possible."

"You say that, but I don't think you're right," Elizabeth replied. "I think you're denying possibilities. After all, all roads lead you to Goddard Downs, and whether you admit it or not, being there means seeing Joshua. Therefore, all roads were leading you to him."

Stella didn't reply. It was pointless to debate. Elizabeth believed what she did, but so did Stella. She spotted the box on the coffee table and decided a change of subject was for the best. "Pizza?"

"Yes, fully loaded," Elizabeth replied with a grin.

Stella flipped the box open, grabbed a slice, and bit into it greedily. If her mouth was full, she couldn't answer any more questions.

CHAPTER 7

*W*hat a day. Frank climbed out of his truck and walked straight into Maggie's waiting arms. It felt so good to hold her after a day filled with more challenges than he'd ever expected.

The sun hovered above the horizon, the sky was the most gorgeous mixture of pinks and purples, and the air was filled with the sound of birds twittering in the trees. It was the best time of day. And not just because of the peace and calm that fell across the land, but because he could come home to Maggie.

"You've had a hard day, Frank. Come inside, and after you're cleaned up, I'll pour us a drink."

He hugged her tight and kissed the top of her head. "Thank you, my love."

She tilted her head upwards and smiled. "You're welcome."

One look at her changed his mood from frustrated to relaxed. Tense to calm. He brushed her hair gently with his hand as he gazed into her eyes. "Some days I'm tempted to go on that trip we've been talking about sooner than later. What would you say to that?"

She chuckled. "I'd be tempted to say yes. But have you forgotten we're going to Darwin soon?"

"That's right. I'm sorry. I did forget. It's those boys. They're driving me crazy." He slipped his arm around her shoulders and together they headed up the steps.

"Did you figure anything out with them?"

"Nope. They've been at each other since they were teenagers, so nothing's going to change overnight."

"That long?"

He nodded as he sat on the top step and pulled his boots off and wiggled his toes.

"I didn't know they fought with each other so much until today. And I didn't know you were aware of it, either."

"Oh, I know, alright. They think they can keep things hidden from me, but I'm they're father, and I know them better than they think."

"Sounds like someone else I know." Maggie chuckled.

"Yep. But He definitely knows everything."

"And He knows how to fix this, too." Maggie joined him on the step and slipped her hand into his.

"You're right. I'm not sure how their issues will be resolved, but somehow God will figure it out."

"Maybe He brought that girl here for a reason. I saw her at church the other week, and I saw the way Joshua looked at her."

Frank sighed. "Maybe. Something's got to give." Placing his other hand over hers, he moved his thumb gently over her soft skin while staring at the darkening horizon. "Joshua was closer to his mother than Julian. Probably because he was the youngest. Her death affected him greatly, and after she passed, he became a risktaker and a rebel, but that's not who he is underneath. I think he's still hurting and trying to figure out his own identity."

"And that's hard to do with Julian in charge."

"Seems that way. Julian always felt that Esther babied Josh too much. I think that's why he's so hard on him. Julian doesn't see the great qualities he has, and vice-versa."

"I guess that's typical of most siblings."

Frank nodded. "Yes, but it doesn't help with the smooth running of the station."

"Things might change if Stella comes on board. She might be the change that's needed. Are you going to employ her?"

"Possibly. We need to discuss it further since we haven't advertised the position. It's going to be a demanding job if we accept Ravi's proposal, and we need to be sure she's up to it."

Maggie squeezed his hand. "There's so much going on, I hope we can still get to Darwin on time."

"Don't worry, my love. We'll get there before the baby's born."

"I'm not worrying, but I think we should pray about it all," she said.

"Good idea. Let's do that." Squeezing her hand, he closed his eyes and began. "Dear Lord, thank You for Your bountiful provisions. You've been watching over this station and our lives for years, meeting our needs, encouraging us to keep going, and for that, we're truly grateful. But we come before You now with heavy hearts. I ask that You intervene in the situation between Julian and Joshua. At their ages they should know better, but ego has come into play, and neither seems prepared to give the other credit for the skills and gifts You've given them. I ask that You soften their hearts and draw them closer to Yourself. And please give us guidance and wisdom with regard to this girl who appeared out of nowhere. Let us know if it's Your will that we employ her, or if she's simply a diversion and You have someone better in mind.

"And I also pray for Serena and David as they look forward to the birth of their baby. Be with them and give them peace, and may the birth go smoothly. And please let Maggie and me get there in time. In Jesus' precious name we pray. Amen."

Maggie continued, her voice soft but steady. "And Lord, I, too, pray for wisdom for Frank as he deals with his sons. You know them better than anyone, and You know what makes them tick. Give Frank insight to know what to say and do to help improve the situation. And lastly, Lord, I want to thank You for bringing Stella here. I don't believe it was a coincidence that she came, but please give Frank and the others peace about employing her. In Your Son's precious name. Amen." She opened her eyes. "Now, Frank Goddard, let me get you that drink."

He chuckled. "Amen to that."

MAGGIE HAD ALREADY prepared Frank's favourite sweet potato bake to accompany the Goddard Downs Angus beef steak they'd cook on the barbecue. After their large midday meal, she didn't need much, but Frank was always hungry, which wasn't surprising considering the physical work he still insisted on doing. They'd fallen into a comfortable routine of eating dinner on the deck while enjoying the cooler evening air after the heat of the day. It was their special time together.

God had blessed them abundantly, but Maggie knew she should never take anything for granted. Things could change in an instant. And so, she'd planned something special for Frank. Knowing how much he treasured his family, she'd spent the last few weeks putting together an audio-visual presentation for him of photos from as far back as she could go. Janella and Olivia had lent her photos they'd taken of their families when they were younger, but she'd also dug into the trunk Frank kept in their room and had come across some really old photos of his parents and grandparents. After collating them she'd set the whole thing to some of his favourite tunes.

While she was working on it, she had no idea of the current problems with Joshua and Julian, so it seemed providential that she'd planned to show it to him tonight. After they ate dinner, she invited him into the loungeroom and asked him to close his eyes.

"Why, whatever for, Maggie?" he asked, a bemused expression on his face as he sank into the leather couch.

"Wait and see," she said with a smile. She had the video ready to go, so she joined him on the couch and turned the television on. Instead of a movie, a picture of the two of them on their wedding day graced the screen. She chuckled in anticipation because she knew Frank would think it was going to be a whole video of their wedding, and she couldn't wait for the photos of his grandparents to show on the screen.

When they did, Frank straightened and looked at her in surprise. "Where did you get these from, Maggie?"

She chuckled and kissed his cheek. "It's a secret. Watch and enjoy."

They settled back together as the history of Goddard Downs played across the screen. Amongst the photos were ones of Esther and the children playing happily together when they were young. Before the boys had begun their tug of war. She prayed silently for peace to once again be restored at Goddard Downs.

After the video finished, Frank took her in his arms and kissed her passionately, the emotion of the display having affected them both. He brushed her lips and whispered words of love, which she whispered back. She was so glad she'd put the video together for him and prayed it would encourage him to trust God to find a solution to the boys' problems.

CHAPTER 8

The following morning, after a relaxed breakfast with Maggie, Frank drove to the homestead to meet with Julian to discuss employing Stella. Frank felt at peace about it, but he sensed Julian was reluctant. Frank would have his job cut out convincing him, but he wasn't alone. As always, God went with him and before him, smoothing the waters, softening hearts, and he had no doubt He was with him now. In fact, as he drove, Frank committed the meeting once again to the Lord.

When he arrived, Isobel and William ran out to greet him. "Have you come to play with us, Grandpa?" Isobel asked, tugging on his hand and looking so adorably cute he could easily have passed on the meeting with Julian. But no. Stella's need was urgent, and employing her would save the hassle of advertising. As far as he was concerned, it was a win-win situation.

"I've got to talk with your Uncle Julian for a while, but then

I can play for a bit."

"Goodie." She jumped up and down. "We'll be in the cubby house."

"Okay. I'll come and find you."

"We'll get a cup of tea ready. And ask Mummy if we can bake a cake."

Frank chuckled. "That sounds great. I'll look forward to it." He ruffled her hair before striding up the stairs.

Julian was in the office and glanced up when Frank entered. He gave a nod. "Morning, Dad."

"And good morning to you, Julian." Frank pulled out a chair and sat on the opposite side of the desk to what he was used to. "No coffee?"

"No. Do you want one?"

"No, it's fine. I know you're busy. Hopefully we can get this over with quickly."

"Have you heard the latest?"

Frank's brow creased. "No. Tell me."

"Joshua and Sean are leaving. They told me this morning."

Frank blew out a breath. "Let me talk with them."

"Good luck with that."

"I don't need good luck. I need wisdom from above."

"You're right. But honestly, Dad, I've had a gut full of them. It's time Joshua grew up."

"And what? Become more like you?"

Julian blinked. "Yes…now you've said it."

"Joshua isn't you, Julian. He's his own person and he has some great qualities."

"I'm glad you think so. I've yet to see them."

"He's going through a rough patch, that's all. I'm sure he'll find himself eventually."

"Rough patch. Is that what you call it? He's wild, Dad. He and Sean together are bad news and I'm happy for them to go."

Frank drew a slow breath. It grieved him to hear his youngest son spoken of in that way, but in many ways, Julian was right. Sean was a bad influence, and the two of them were almost joined at the hip. Frank wasn't sure what it would take for Joshua to mend his ways, but he believed that God would reach deep inside his heart and draw him back to Himself. He didn't know how or when He'd do it, but Frank had confidence that He would.

"If they go, who'd take over the cattle drives?"

Julian gave a lopsided grin. "You and Maggie?"

Frank's brows arched in surprise. "No…"

Julian nodded. "Why not? You'd be perfect for the job."

"I'm not sure Maggie would agree, but I'll talk it over with her, although I hope it won't come to that. Also, we'll be heading to Darwin soon, so I'm not sure it will work. I'll talk to Joshua."

"Okay. But don't leave it too long. They're planning on leaving after this drive."

"That soon?"

Julian nodded again. "Anyway, we're supposed to be talking about the vet position."

"Yes," Frank said. "Have you read her résumé?"

Julian leaned back in his chair and cracked his knuckles. "I have. It's impressive. But don't you think it's too much of a coincidence that she turned up like she did? How did she know about Simon retiring? We haven't advertised the position yet."

"I don't know, and I don't think it really matters," Frank said. "She's highly qualified and we need a vet. As far as I can see, it's a no-brainer. Plus, she needs the work." He went on to explain to Julian the dire predicament the Martins were in.

Julian's face paled. "I had no idea they were in such strife. But it sounds like it's too late if the bank's already foreclosed."

"It may well be, but she's determined to do her best to save Indigo, or buy it back, if that's the only option."

"How would she save enough money before someone else snaps it up? It'll probably go for a song."

"With the uncertainty over the live cattle exports, stations aren't selling too well these days. You know that, son."

Julian sighed heavily. "Yes, I do know that."

"We've been very blessed. The deal with Ravi Tamala, along with the cattle drives, got us out of trouble. And now, with this new deal of Ravi's on the table, I think we'll be set for a long time to come."

"And that brings us back to Stella. Do you really think she's capable of handling the job, especially with the extra cattle we'll be running?"

"I do. I truly do. And I think we should offer it to her."

"Without a formal interview?"

Frank nodded. "We can put her on a trial. We'll know quickly if she's up to it or not."

"Especially if we give her the back paddock to look after first." Julian's eyes twinkled. Goddard Downs' largest, meanest bull lived in the back paddock, and even the men were wary of going near the brute. The bull, however, was due for his annual inoculations and check-up.

"That's not fair, Julian," Frank said.

Julian chuckled. "I know. But if she can handle him, the job's hers."

Frank stuck his hand out across the desk. "Deal."

Julian shook it. "I hope we don't regret this."

"We won't." Frank pushed to his feet. "I've got to run. I've got a play date and a cup of tea waiting for me in the cubby house."

"Some of us have all the fun." Julian shook his head, but Frank was pleased to see a grin on his face.

"You should try it sometime." He gave Julian a wink before heading out the door. He poked his head back in quickly. "By the way, since you're the boss, I think it should be you who gives Stella the news."

"I was planning on it."

Frank smiled. "Good. And I'll talk with Joshua first chance I get."

"I won't hold my breath."

"Best not. But don't worry. One way or another, we'll figure it all out."

"I'm glad you're confident."

"I have confidence in the Lord, and that's the most important thing." Frank gave another nod and then headed outside to find his grandchildren.

JULIAN PUT his head in his hands and groaned. His dad was incorrigible. Why did he always get his way? It was so annoying. He wasn't in charge anymore, but he had a way of turning things around to get what he wanted. And his faith put Julian's to shame. Julian believed, but his day-to-day walk with God was feeble in comparison to his dad's. Could he ever become like him? Some days, like today, he doubted it.

Sighing, he lifted the receiver and dialled Stella's number, while praying silently he was doing the right thing.

CHAPTER 9

hree days later, Stella parked her Toyota Hilux outside the main homestead at Goddard Downs after an emotional farewell with her parents. They'd left that morning for Cootamundra, a trip that would take them several days, while she headed in the opposite direction, to Goddard Downs—a much shorter trip. Three hours, to be exact, but she'd taken it slowly, so it took closer to four.

While she was thrilled that her audacity had paid off and she'd been offered the job as the large animal vet on the station, a flicker of apprehension coursed through her as she'd driven along the dusty, rutted road. The grader hadn't been through in a while, and the corrugations in the road seemed to have grown worse in the few days since she'd last driven it. Several larger four-wheel drive vehicles had overtaken her, and each time she'd had to slow down even more to let the dust settle. The drivers obviously had no consideration for their fellow travellers.

As she turned off the main road and headed up the track that led to Goddard Downs, she slowed even further and took in her surroundings. It was beautiful country. A mixture of vast savannah plains framed by the dark, jagged outlines of the Mirima mountain range, and cool, shaded creek crossings that were now dry, but would soon gush with life-giving water once the rainy season began.

Livestock grazing on the sparse vegetation dotted the plains. Goddard Downs ran 5,000 head of Brahman cross cattle spread over their 150,000 acres. That was a lot of cattle to look after. Much more than the thousand head they'd run at Indigo. Tears sprang to her eyes as she recalled the heartache she and her parents had felt as the final truckload of their precious cattle disappeared into a cloud of dust. They had remained watching long after the dust settled and the truck was out of sight.

Now, nothing was left but memories. But she'd get it back. One way or another, Indigo would once again belong to the Martin family. She didn't know how long it would take, or how she would accumulate enough money to buy it back, but this job was a start. And although it meant working alongside Joshua, she'd do it with a glad heart. God had opened the door for her, and she was grateful for His provision. If only He'd calm the butterflies in her stomach.

She'd half expected Joshua to be there when she arrived, but was relieved when he wasn't. Not that she didn't like the guy. He was good-looking and fun to be around, and she had fond memories of the time they'd spent together in Alice Springs at the rodeo. But he was too wild for her. Not that she was looking for a boyfriend. But if she was, she'd want a man who shared her faith. Joshua might hail from a Christian family, but she'd gotten the impression that he himself wasn't a believer. Or perhaps he was simply rebelling. That happened. And God was more than capable of wooing His children back into the fold. But it was of no consequence. She wasn't interested in a relationship, with Joshua Goddard or anyone else, and she'd make that clear at the first opportunity. Which wasn't now, because it was Frank who'd come out to greet her. She acknowledged his smile with a wave as he approached her vehicle. But then Joshua appeared from the other direction, seemingly oblivious to her presence, until he stopped in his tracks, his eyes bulging.

He wore faded jeans, boots, and a white shirt with sleeves rolled to his elbows. It was also open at his neck and revealed dark, manly chest hair. But it wasn't his attire that made her breath catch. It was his crystal-clear eyes, the ones that had captivated her when they first met, and the day-old stubble on his face. He was way too handsome. She gulped hard and gathered her emotions. She had no interest in him, even if her insides tingled at the mere sight of him. It was nothing more than physical attraction. Not nearly enough to build a relationship on. Not that she was seeking a relationship, she reminded herself firmly.

"Stella!" Frank said, smiling. "Great to see you. I hope you had a good trip."

"Yes, thanks. It was fine. No dramas."

"Good to hear. Julian gives his apologies. He got entangled in a business meeting in town and won't be back until later this afternoon."

She smiled. "That's fine. I'm sure we'll catch up in due

course."

"Yes. He'll be here for when you officially start in the morning. I think he's already got a job lined up for you."

"Sounds good. I'm excited to get started."

"And we're pleased to have you here. So, would you like to see your quarters first, or would you like a drink?"

She held up her water container. "I've been drinking the whole way. I'd love to see my quarters."

"Great. Joshua here can show you around, can't you, Josh?" Frank turned and motioned for him to join them. "I've heard you two might already know each other."

Stella tried her hardest to avoid looking directly at him, but it was impossible. Their gazes met briefly, and once again her stomach fizzed as she looked into his eyes that were as clear as a mountain stream. She quickly chastised herself for her reaction. "Not really," she said, her voice coming out not as firm as she would have liked. *Why didn't she simply come out and say they knew each other?* The effect he had on her was beyond rational. He'd captivated her, there was no doubt about it. But she wouldn't allow him to get under her skin and weave his way into her heart. No. She was stronger than that.

"Stella." Joshua offered a cursory, almost dismissive nod. She didn't blame him. She should have acknowledged they were acquainted. "The staff quarters are down there, a few hundred metres." He pointed to his right, between a large shed and holding stables where several horses were tethered to the rail. "Best if you drive."

"Sure. Do you want a ride?"

"Thanks, but I'll walk."

"Okay." She turned to Frank. "Will I catch you later?"

"Probably. I think the women are planning a welcome dinner for you."

She angled her head, her brows scrunching. "Really?"

"Yes. Everyone wants to meet you."

"That's very kind."

"We like to make our staff feel welcome."

"I'll look forward to it. Thank you, Frank."

"Our pleasure. I hope your quarters are satisfactory."

"I'm sure they will be." She smiled again. Frank had the same crystal-clear, blue eyes as his son, but he was a lot more agreeable.

She climbed back into her Jeep and started the engine, giving a wave to Frank as she headed in the direction Joshua was walking. When she caught up with him, she stopped and asked again if he wanted a lift.

Their gazes locked for a moment before he opened the door and jumped in. Acutely aware of his close presence, her heart involuntarily picked up its pace as his manly aroma filled the vehicle.

"Why didn't you mention we knew each other?" Facing her, he pinned her with those bright eyes.

She shrank under his gaze. "I honestly don't know."

"And what about my calls? I thought we were friends." His accusing gaze was riveted on her.

She sat back, momentarily rebuffed. "We are." Her voice was soft, apologetic. "I've just been really busy since I left Alice."

"Too busy to answer my calls?"

She winced. "I'm sorry. I didn't know what to say."

"Hello would have been a good start."

She swallowed hard. "You're right. It was rude of me to ignore you."

When he spoke again, his words were measured. Almost angry. "No saying?"

"I'm sorry, Joshua. I really am."

He clenched his mouth tighter. "Well, you're here now. We'd better at least be civil."

Without thinking, she reached out and touched his arm. "We can be more than civil. We can be friends."

He puffed out a big breath. "I'm not quite sure what that means, but okay. I guess we can be friends."

She felt terrible. She'd been rude, and she knew it. She also sensed that he wanted more than she was offering.

JOSHUA GLANCED sideways at Stella as she concentrated on driving her Jeep down the rutted track towards the staff quarters. She was still as gorgeous as ever, and with her so close, he couldn't ignore the effect she had on him, but what was she playing at? *Did she really think that all he wanted was friendship?* If she'd given any indication she was interested in him, he would have instantly declared his feelings. *But friendship?* How could they live so close and simply be friends? It would have been better if Dad hadn't convinced him to stay. If he and Sean had kept to their plans, they'd be in Kununurra by now, if not Darwin. And then he wouldn't be in this untenable situation.

Could he be satisfied with friendship? He honestly didn't know.

She stopped the car when they reached the staff quarters, a simple dwelling consisting of a number of single rooms, which although small, were comfortably furnished. Most of the staff shared the bathrooms and kitchen, but as head vet, Stella had a larger unit with her own ensuite, kitchenette, and a small living area. Simon, the retiring vet, and his wife, Sara had already vacated the unit and were living in their camper until they left in a day's time.

"The quarters look nice," Stella said, opening the car door and jumping out.

Josh struggled to keep his eyes off her. She was wearing khaki shorts and a matching shirt. Typical vet attire, but with her long, shapely, tanned legs, the outfit looked hot.

He cleared his throat. "I guess you were told you'd have a unit."

"Yes. Your brother mentioned that. I told him I didn't need much space, but he insisted I have it."

Joshua grabbed two bags from her back seat and carried them up several stairs before setting them down on the small porch while he opened the door. "This is it." He stepped aside so she could see in.

"It's lovely." She walked past him carrying a bag, and he inhaled the scent of her freshly washed hair.

He took the bags inside, then went back for the remaining two. After setting them down, he shoved his hands in his pockets. "Do you want to unpack or would you like a tour?"

"I'd love a tour. I can unpack anytime." Her brows creased. "But don't you have things to do?"

He shuffled his feet. "Yeah, but nothing that can't wait."

"So long as you're sure."

He was sure of only one thing. Stella Martin had stolen his heart.

CHAPTER 10

*J*oshua waited outside while Stella freshened up, his jaw tense. Dad had dropped him in this, big time. Instead of taking Stella Martin on a grand tour of Goddard Downs, Joshua should have been helping Sean prepare for tomorrow's cattle drive. Julian should have been here to look after her, but of course, he wasn't. Typical. Joshua folded his arms and slumped against Stella's Jeep. The whole universe seemed to be conspiring against him. Stella was here. That was a dream come true. But she only wanted to be friends.

How could they simply be friends? What was wrong with him that made her not want anything more than friendship? He didn't understand. They'd been close in Alice. He was sure she felt something for him then. From the way she'd clung to him while they'd danced, he'd gotten the impression she at least liked him. He should have said something then. *Why hadn't he said something?*

A heavy sigh escaped his lips. Would he ever get to make his own decisions? Get to do what he wanted? Somehow, he doubted it. He couldn't even get the girl he wanted.

She stepped out onto the small deck. He straightened, his breath catching. She was drop dead gorgeous. She bounced down the three steps and joined him. "I'm ready. Are we driving or riding?"

He cleared his throat. "You don't want to see the clinic first?"

"I can see it tomorrow. Right now, I'd love to see the cattle."

"Okay. Your choice. Would you prefer to drive or ride?"

"I'd love to ride, if that's alright." Her eyes were bright, as if she were trying to smooth things between them.

"That's fine. We can grab some horses. They're just up the track a bit."

"Great." She flicked some hair over her shoulder as they began walking. "It's lovely here. I like it already."

"Yeah. It's not bad. Sorry to hear about your place."

She blew out a heavy breath and gave a small smile. "Thanks. It's been a hard few months. But this job is an answer to prayer."

He ignored her last comment. If her coming here was an answer to prayer, God had a strange sense of humour. "Your parents have gone south?"

"Yes. To Cootamundra. My mother's family is down there. My parents lost all hope and stopped fighting to keep the station. I'm going to get it back for them."

His head snapped around. "How are you going to do that?"

She shrugged. "I don't know, but God does."

He groaned. Could he never escape religious talk? Wasn't it

enough that Dad and his siblings talked about God all the time? But Stella, too? Maybe it was for the best she didn't want anything to do with him. He didn't need another saint in his life.

They reached the shed where two horses were tethered out front. He dashed inside and grabbed the saddles. "You can take this horse." He put one of the saddles on a chestnut mare.

"What's her name? She's a beauty." Stella gave the horse a close inspection, running her hand gently across the horse's side.

"Brandy." He handed her the reins.

"Thanks." She mounted the horse with ease while he mounted Flame, his three-year-old black colt. "Which way?" she asked after settling into her saddle.

"We can go to the top paddock and check out some of the cattle, then come back along the ridge and stop by the back paddock where Brutus hangs out." He lifted the reins and his horse responded.

Stella followed suit. "Brutus? I'm guessing he's not the friendliest of bulls."

"You got it in one."

"Bulls don't worry me. You just have to call their bluff."

Joshua shook his head. She had no idea what she was in for. He was a bull-riding cowboy, and even he didn't get too close to Brutus.

They increased the pace to a slow trot. Stella looked comfortable in the saddle. In fact, she looked more than comfortable. She rode like a pro. Which of course, she was. Growing up on a cattle station, there was really no choice but to become a proficient rider.

After leaving the shaded homestead area, the afternoon sun bore down on their backs as the horses picked up their pace and they headed towards the top paddock. Most of the Goddard Downs' cattle roamed free across the 150,000 acres. Only the cattle used in the tourist drives, or those about to give birth or needing treatment, were kept in the paddocks closer to the homestead.

The regular rhythm of his horse's gallop was a balm to Joshua's troubled heart. Nothing could beat galloping across the open countryside, wind whipping through his hair, drying the sweat from his brow. Even having Stella beside him couldn't steal the exhilaration he felt.

They arrived at the top paddock and slowed the horses to a walk.

"That was fun," she said. Her face glistened and her cheeks were pink.

"Yep. Nothing better than a good ride to blow the cobwebs away."

Their gazes connected and his pulse quickened. A groan escaped him. Why did she have this effect on him?

The moment ended, and he swung his gaze to the herd of cattle grazing near some boab trees.

"They look healthy," she said, nodding in their direction.

"Yeah. They're the ones we use for the drives. They're pretty sedate."

"Do you enjoy doing the drives?" She removed her hat and wiped her brow with her forearm.

He shrugged. "Some are better than others. Depends on the people."

"I guess so. I imagine you get some difficult clients."

"You could say that." He grabbed a couple of water bottles from his saddle bag and tossed her one.

"Thanks." She smiled as she caught it and drank half the bottle before handing it back.

"We can go higher if you want. There's a nice view from the ridge."

"Sounds good. I'll race you." She took off and he had trouble catching her. But he did, finally, just before they reached the top. When they both stopped, he shook his head and laughed. "You're a wild one. I thought you'd ride slower."

She laughed back. "What made you think that?"

He shrugged. "Don't know." He gulped. Oh, he wanted to hold her like he'd held her that night in Alice. *How had it not meant anything to her?* He closed his eyes and remembered the feel of her body against his as they swayed to a Keith Urban slow number. He had to get out of here. Being around her was no good. "Come on. I've got to get back."

Her forehead creased. "So soon?"

"I just remembered. I'm supposed to be helping Sean."

"Your cousin? The one with you in Alice?"

"Yeah. That's him."

"I didn't know he was here."

"He does the drives with me, but we're leaving as soon as the rains hit."

"Oh? Where are you going?"

"I don't know." He kicked Flame harder than he should and the horse responded, reaching a gallop in no time at all. He breathed heavily as the horse pounded across the dry land.

What had he done? What had made him behave so immaturely? It was as if he'd lost control of his words and actions.

He hadn't meant to talk to Stella like that. Leave her with her mouth gaping as he sped off. He reined the horse in and stopped, needing to apologise.

PUZZLED, Stella watched Joshua gallop away. What just happened? One moment they'd been chatting easily, the next, he was off like a rocket, leaving her all alone. It didn't make sense. And then it did.

With clarity that only came from the Lord, she realised that he was fighting a battle, not only with himself, but with God. Hanging around with his cousin wasn't helping him. From what she'd seen of the guy in Alice, he wasn't a good influence. He liked his drink, and he liked the women. Joshua was torn. Although he'd said that he and Sean were leaving the station, she sensed that underneath, he didn't want to. Sean was causing him to be unsettled. Tempting him with a different life.

She offered up a prayer for them both as she sped after Joshua. She could just make him out in the distance. It looked like he'd stopped and was waiting for her. She urged Brandy on, but as she neared, two other horses approached from the opposite direction. It looked like Frank, and a woman, Stella assumed, was his wife.

She slowed and stopped beside Joshua moments before the couple reached them. There was not enough time to discuss what had just happened, but there was an almost imperceptible note of pleading on Joshua's face. But what was he pleading for? Forgiveness? Or something else? For her to tell him not to leave? That she wanted to be more than just friends? She shook her head. It would be too easy to fall for him. His rugged handsomeness made her heart beat faster, and despite his erratic behaviour, she knew he was a good man. But she couldn't allow herself to fall in love. She was here for one reason only. To save Indigo.

Pushing the events of the past few moments aside, Stella smiled warmly as Frank took his hat off and introduced his wife. Any discussion between her and Joshua would have to wait.

"SHE SEEMS A LOVELY YOUNG WOMAN," Maggie said to Frank after they left Joshua and Stella and continued their ride. "And fancy knowing her! Do you think something could be going on? I caught a few glances between them. I have a feeling they know each other better than they're letting on."

"Maggie!" Frank let out a deep belly laugh as he shook his head.

She glanced at the pair still sitting astride their horses, deep in conversation. A smile lifted her lips. "They make a handsome couple."

Frank shook his head again, but there was a sparkle in his eye. "Match making again. I don't know how you come up with these things, my love." He reached across and squeezed her hand. "But if Stella Martin is the reason Joshua stays at Goddard Downs, I won't complain."

"Maybe God's brought her for a reason other than simply being the vet."

Frank inhaled deeply. "You might be right. It'd be good for Josh to settle down with someone, but not just anyone. Someone who loves the Lord. It's every Christian parent's prayer that their offspring find love with a fellow believer. I just don't know if Josh believes anymore."

"Oh, Frank." The sadness in her husband's voice reached deep inside Maggie. She knew intimately the despair he was feeling, but Serena was living proof that God was able to do abundantly above all that she'd ever asked or thought, and He could do the same in Joshua's life.

"He hasn't been the same since Esther passed away. I have to take some of the blame for how he is now, because at the time, I was more concerned about Caleb and Sasha than him since they were younger. But Esther's passing affected him greatly."

"He's probably internalised his emotions. Men often don't talk about how they feel."

Frank nodded. "I think you're right. He seemed so stoic at the time, and I can't recall him shedding a tear. But neither did Julian, although that shouldn't have surprised me."

"Maybe you should try and talk to Josh about it. See if he'll open up."

He faced her and smiled. "I will. Thank you for being here, Maggie. My life is so much richer with you in it."

She met his kind, gentle gaze and tears pricked her eyes. How blessed she was to have him in her life. "Oh Frank. You're such a softie. And you know what? I think Joshua is exactly like you underneath. He just needs to have his protective layers peeled back. Would you like to stop and pray for him?"

"That would be wonderful."

They stopped under the shade of a boab tree and took in the breathtaking vista. Vast, open plains dotted with boabs, grazing cattle, and wallabies lazing in the afternoon sun. Rich, ochre outlines of the mountain range in the distance, contrasting with the deep blue of the endless sky. God's amazing handiwork, reflecting His love for mankind.

Maggie squeezed Frank's hand. "Shall we?"

He nodded, and bowing her head, Maggie began. "Lord God, Your creation is beyond comprehension, and we acknowledge and are humbled by Your supreme love for mankind. That You could love us so much that not only did You create all of this for our benefit, but that even while we were deep in sin, You sent Your Son to die on the cross so we could be freed from that sin and live with You forever.

"Lord God, we pray for Joshua right now. He's a troubled young man, but we know that You can reach deep inside his heart and release him from the wounds that have been festering for years, and fill him with peace and purpose. We don't know if Stella is part of Your plan for Joshua, but thank You for bringing her here. We ask that You bless her and her family as they deal with the loss of their family home and livelihood. And Lord, I pray that You'll give Frank wisdom as he speaks with Joshua. Give him words that will reach beneath the surface of his crusty exterior and allow them to connect in a meaningful way. Lord, we thank You for Your abundant mercy and love. Thank You for the love that Frank and I have for each other. We're so blessed that You brought us together. In Jesus' precious name we pray. Amen."

Frank continued. "Lord, forgive me for not giving Joshua the attention he needed. I blame myself for his wild ways, but

Lord, You're in the business of mending hearts and lives, and I know You can mend Josh's. And Lord, I once again bring the feud between him and Julian to You. Please intervene and help them to set their egos aside and learn to get on with each other as You would want them to do. In Your Son's name. Amen."

CHAPTER 11

*J*oshua's gaze stayed fixed on his dad and Maggie as they continued their ride. The conversation between the four had been pleasant, especially when Maggie said she recognised Stella from church. Both his father and Stella had been surprised by Maggie's observation, but Joshua hadn't been. Stella was unforgettable, at least in his eyes.

He'd tried to engage in the conversation and not allow any of the emotions bubbling inside him to seep out, but now, he could feel Stella's gaze on him. She wanted to know why he'd raced off like he did.

But he couldn't tell her. It was obvious she didn't like him, not in the way he wanted, and he'd feel a fool if he were to bare his heart only to have it rejected. No, it was better to make up some nonsense and leave it at that. Pulling on his horse's reins, he turned and faced her, blew out a breath and curled a hand behind his neck. "Sorry about before, but I do need to get back and help Sean. He'll be wondering where I am."

"Okay…" Her eyes narrowed. She didn't believe him, but what did it matter?

He moved the horse on and Stella followed. Soon they were riding side by side, fast enough to make conversation difficult, but not fast enough for him to not be acutely aware of her presence beside him. He'd never had a steady girlfriend, but he could imagine how nice it would be to ride like this with someone you loved. Like Dad and Maggie were doing. At first, he hadn't liked the idea of his dad remarrying. How could he replace Mum with someone else? But Maggie seemed nice enough and his dad seemed happy. How could Joshua begrudge him that?

Stella slowed, and pointing to her right, called out, "Is that Brutus?"

Joshua peered in the direction she was pointing. Yes, the brute was up there. He nodded as he reined his horse in and trotted alongside Stella. "Do you want to check him out?"

"I thought you had to get back."

"I do. But a few more minutes won't matter."

"Okay. Let's go."

The truth was, he didn't want to leave her. Yes, he did need to get back and help Sean, and yes, being with her was causing all sorts of internal turmoil, but he simply wanted to be near her, even if he couldn't have her. She was like a magnet, and he had no resistance. "We'll approach slowly, and it's best we stay on the horses. We can outrun him if he charges."

"Is he really that bad?"

Joshua chuckled. "You'd better believe it." He pointed his horse towards the hollow where Brutus was standing. The two-thousand-pound prize Brahman bull had seen them already and was stomping the ground with his front hoof.

"Maybe we should leave it. I don't want to upset him unnecessarily, especially since I'll be seeing him tomorrow."

Joshua shrugged. "Your call."

"I'm happy to head back. I'm starting to feel a bit weary."

For the first time, he noticed the shadows under her eyes and felt bad that he hadn't given much thought about what had brought her to Goddard Downs in the first place. "I guess it's been a big day for you."

"It has. But I'm happy to be here. I really think I'm going to enjoy it."

"You and Maggie seemed to hit it off."

"Yes. It's funny, though. With all the stuff happening at home, I haven't been going to church often. She must have seen me the one time I went a few weeks ago."

"I used to go before Mum died."

"You haven't been since?" Stella's voice was soft, tender.

He shook his head. "Nuh. It's too far."

Her brows lifted. "Is that the only reason?"

He chuckled. He should have known she'd see through his weak excuse. "No. I just don't see much benefit in going."

"Church isn't everything, but I find that meeting with other believers is a real encouragement."

He sighed heavily and stared into the distance across the vast, open plains. "I'm not sure if I believe anymore."

"What caused you to start doubting?"

He shrugged. "I don't know, really. It was probably soon after Mum died. It seemed unfair that she died trying to rescue her grandkids. It made me start thinking that if God was as powerful as we'd been told He was, why didn't He save Mum when she was trying to save others?"

Stella drew a slow breath. "There's no easy answer to that. A lot of people struggle with that same question, and my only explanation is that God sees a bigger picture to what we see, but one day, everything will become clear. In the meantime, He gives us strength to face whatever challenges come our way, including deaths of loved ones. And losses of family homes."

He swung his gaze to her. "Aren't you bitter about losing it?"

She took a moment, and when she looked at him again, her eyes were moist. "I've been struggling with it, yes. I don't think it's fair we lost it."

"It must have been horrible. I can't imagine losing Goddard Downs." As much as he wanted to get away, he'd be devastated if his family suffered the same fate as Stella's. He'd never known any other home and couldn't imagine his family living anywhere else. This land was in his blood, even if sometimes he felt he couldn't breathe. But that was more Julian's doing than anything else.

"It hasn't been easy, but I'm determined to get it back." She blinked and quickly brushed her eyes with the back of her hand.

He admired her determination, but the likelihood of getting the station back was slim. A savvy investor would snap it up and it'd be gone. He also wondered where her faith came in since her earlier statement seemed at odds with her resolve.

Without thinking, he asked, "And what if you don't? What if God doesn't want you to get it back?"

Her whole body stiffened, and he immediately chastised himself for asking such a confrontational question.

"He has to," she whispered, her voice fragile. "Indigo is my life."

Joshua simply nodded. It was obvious she'd not allowed herself to entertain the idea that she might not get it back, and he wondered how she'd cope if she didn't. Would she still believe? He gave an apologetic smile. "I'm sorry. I shouldn't have asked that."

She flicked some hair off her shoulder. "It's okay. I just hadn't considered that as an option, that's all."

She was struggling with stuff, too. Maybe they weren't so different after all. "Come on. Let's head back." He lifted his reins and Flame responded. When the homestead came into view, he slowed the horse and steered him towards the staff accommodation area. Sean was loading the truck as they passed the shed. He looked up, his eyes narrowing.

Joshua brought Flame to a halt. Stella reined in her horse and stopped beside him.

An awkward silence followed before Joshua cleared his throat. "Sorry, mate. I got a bit caught up. You remember Stella?"

Sean nodded, a fake smile plastered on his face. "Of course. Nice to see you again."

"And you, Sean." Stella's smile was warm, which was surprising because she and Sean hadn't gotten on too well in Alice. "Joshua's been giving me a quick tour of the place."

"So I can see. What happened to Julian?" Sean quirked a brow at Joshua.

"Got held up in town."

"And you happily stepped in." There was an edge to his voice.

Joshua gritted his teeth. He liked his cousin, but he didn't like the jealous streak that came out whenever Joshua showed anyone else attention, particularly Stella. Sean didn't seem to realise, however, that he had double standards. He had no qualms about leaving Joshua and going off with any girl who caught his attention, but he didn't like it when Joshua did the same. But he shouldn't have left Sean to prepare for the cattle drive without telling him he'd be delayed. "I'll drop Stella back and come and help."

"No need," Stella said. "I can find my own way." She dismounted her horse and handed him the reins.

Joshua looked at her apologetically. "Sorry."

"It's fine. Thanks for the tour. I enjoyed it." As their gazes held, she gave a smile that tortured him. His feelings towards her were intensifying quickly. If only she felt the same about him.

He nodded. "Okay. I'll catch you later."

"Hey," Sean called after her as she headed off. "There's a party tonight. Why don't you come?"

Joshua glared at him. Sean's tone was filled with sarcasm and derision. He knew Stella wouldn't go to a party, particularly one he was organising. He was simply stirring things up, but Stella didn't seem perturbed. Turning, she thanked him but declined, saying she was planning an early night after the welcome dinner.

"Yeah, I guess you need your beauty sleep."

Joshua jumped off his horse and shoved Sean in the chest. "Quit it, will you?"

"Touchy, touchy."

Joshua inhaled deeply before tethering the horses to the rail and grabbing a bale of hay and tossing it onto the truck.

CHAPTER 12

*A*lthough she was grateful the family wanted to welcome her, Stella would have preferred that early night she'd told Sean she was planning. She didn't know Sean well, but from what she'd seen of him in Alice, she didn't like him, or at least, she didn't like the hold he had on Joshua. It surprised her that Joshua still hung out with him.

But she had to attend the dinner. It would be rude not to. She stepped into the shower to freshen up, and the cool water quickly revived her body, but as she adjusted the temperature up and her thoughts turned to the question Joshua had posed, her insides tensed. What if God didn't want her to get Indigo back? The thought made her feel ill. It couldn't be possible. It *was* His will. He'd brought her here and given her this job so she could raise the funds to buy it back. She was trusting Him.

A verse she'd memorised years before at Sunday school crossed her mind. *But seek first the Kingdom of God and His righteousness, and all these things shall be added to you.*

"I *am* seeking Your Kingdom first, Lord," she insisted aloud, her shoulders squared. But something inside made her question the truth of that.

Pushing those thoughts to the back of her mind, she shut the shower off, dried herself, and then rummaged through her suitcase to find something suitable to wear. Since her wardrobe was filled mainly with charity store clothing and work uniforms, the choices were limited. One day she'd have enough money to buy a new outfit, but for now, it was a choice between a cool, midi-length summer dress with shoe-string straps, or her trusty pair of jeans and white shirt. With the heat still oppressive, she chose the dress, despite not being overly fond of its chocolate-brown colour. There was little she could do to liven the dress up, so she tied a multi-coloured scarf around her head, hooked a pair of dangly earrings into her ears, and applied some mascara and a touch of lip gloss.

Looking in the mirror and not liking what she saw, she reminded herself of what her grandmother used to say... *Outward appearances don't matter, Stella. It's what's on the inside that counts.*

But she wanted to look nice tonight. Although she wouldn't encourage Joshua, she couldn't deny the fact that her heart turned over in response every time their gazes met. It wasn't only his rugged handsomeness that drew her. She'd seen glimpses of his caring nature when they were in Alice, when he'd helped a young boy who'd been wandering around, distraught, searching for his parents, when he'd helped her tend to an injured steer, and when he'd held her while they danced...

She blinked. No, she wouldn't go there. Once again, her

grandmother's words came to mind. *Stella, think carefully about whom you choose as your life partner. Don't let yourself fall for just anyone. It's so easy to fall in love, but it's not so easy to stay in love, especially when things get tough. Choose someone who has the same trust in the Lord as you do. Who's going after the same things. Although nothing's guaranteed, there's more likelihood of a marriage lasting the distance if you start off as friends and get to know each other before you even kiss. As soon as you cross that line, it's hard to go back.*

Yes, it would be very hard to go back. She couldn't even think about kissing Joshua Goddard without her heart racing. What would it do if she actually kissed him? *Oh, Lord, please help me to stay strong and keep my resolve to only be friends with Joshua.*

A knock sounded on the door. She took a deep breath, and after grabbing her denim jacket from the back of the chair where she'd put it earlier, she gingerly opened the door. She was half expecting it to be Joshua and was disappointed when it wasn't. The man standing on the doorstep had to be his brother. The clear blue eyes were a giveaway.

He extended his hand. "Stella. It's nice to meet you face to face. I'm Julian."

She smiled and shook his hand. "And it's nice to meet you." She followed him to his truck. "I could have walked."

"I know, but since it's your first day and I missed giving you the tour, picking you up was the least I could do."

"Well, thank you. I appreciate it."

He held the door open for her while she climbed in. "I hope that brother of mine looked after you in my absence," he said after he jumped in the driver's side.

"Yes, he gave me a good tour. From what I saw, it's a wonderful property."

"We love it, but I guess we're biased. Did you happen to meet Brutus?" He shot her a sidewise glance.

"Briefly. I believe he's my first job tomorrow."

"Yes. Do you think you're up to it?" His tone wasn't unfriendly, but it was enough to make her bristle.

She straightened. "I believe I am." There was no hiding the fact that Julian doubted her capabilities. She'd sensed the job had only been offered to her because Frank had vouched for her, but now she was convinced that was definitely the case. She'd have to prove herself to his son. Would she ever be good enough in his eyes, since no doubt he would have preferred a male vet? But she was up to it. She'd graduated top of her year at university, and although other than the position she'd snagged at the rodeo, she'd only worked on her family cattle station. There, she'd faced the whole gamut of situations vets handled on larger cattle stations, including dealing with feisty bulls.

"I guess we'll see." He gave a polite smile as he stopped the truck in front of the homestead. "Have you met everyone yet?"

"No. Only Joshua, Frank and Maggie." She omitted mentioning Sean on purpose.

"Okay. Time to meet the others."

She smiled. "I'm looking forward to it." After climbing out of the truck, she stood for a moment and took in the scene. Several tables had been set up on a patch of green grass on the shady side of the homestead. The patch was obviously well cared for since everything around it was dry and dusty. Two rows of fairy lights hung between the house and the gum trees, and although it wasn't yet fully dark, the sparkling lights made the area cosy and inviting. The aroma of barbecuing meat wafted in the air, reminding her she hadn't told anyone she was vegetarian.

She inhaled deeply and walked with her chin up beside Julian towards a group of three women who were standing together, talking. Maggie was amongst the group, and Stella guessed that the other two were Frank's daughter and daughter-in-law. She was right. Julian introduced them as his sister, Olivia, and his wife, Janella. They both greeted her with a smile and a hug and welcomed her to Goddard Downs. Maggie stood back, but then also greeted her with a hug.

Julian offered to get her a drink.

"Water will be fine," she said.

He returned moments later with a large glass and handed it to her.

She smiled and thanked him, and quickly looked around to see if she could spot Joshua, but he wasn't there. A twinge of disappointment flowed through her. Maybe he was still coming.

"I'm sorry to hear about Indigo," Janella said.

Stella blinked and then quickly nodded. "Thank you. It was really hard saying goodbye."

"I can imagine," Janella said. "I've lived here most of my life, and it would be so hard to leave."

"Really? That's a surprise!"

"Yes. My family came here when I was young. My dad was head stockman."

"Oh." Stella immediately thought of Daku and all the other workers who'd left Indigo to find other work and homes. The cattle station's demise had impacted a lot of people and she felt bad about that. But what intrigued her was that the eldest Goddard son had married the stockman's daughter. Janella was an attractive woman, a few inches shorter than her sister-in-law, who was probably five-ten, and also a little plumper, and her round face was friendly and her dark eyes, soft. That she had indigenous blood was evident from the colour of her skin, the same shade as Stella's dress. In her experience, few land owners approved of their children marrying someone from a different culture, particularly the indigenous one, but it seemed that Frank and his first wife must have, and that raised Stella's opinion of him even more. Some of the aborigines in the area did cause trouble, but many were hard, loyal workers who cared deeply for their families. Daku was a prime example, and so, it seemed, was Janella's father. "I can understand how hard it would be to leave in that case. Not that you'll have to. I've heard only good things about Goddard Downs."

"Thank you. We've all worked hard to keep it going, especially during the ban, but we have to give God the thanks. We could have so easily gone under."

Stella's smile remained fixed, but Janella's last statement stung. Why had God saved Goddard Downs and not Indigo? Did He have something against her and her family? While she knew those thoughts were nonsense and God had His reasons, she couldn't help asking the question. Much like Joshua had questioned why his mother had been lost when the children had been saved. Did God have favourites? Those He listened to more than others? How did He choose who lived and who died, or what stations survived and which went under? If only she could understand His thinking.

"For My thoughts are not your thoughts, nor are your ways My ways," says the Lord. "For as the heavens are higher than the earth, so are My ways higher than your ways, and My thoughts than your thoughts."

Stella turned her gaze to the darkening horizon splattered with colours, rich and vibrant, and all of a sudden, a sense of God's majesty and power swept through her. Who indeed was she to question His ways? He was the Creator of heaven and earth, and she was a mere mortal.

I love you, Stella, and want the best for you. But seek Me first.

She gulped. There it was again. *I am seeking You first, Lord. You know I am.*

"Hey, Stella. Good to see you again." She turned at the familiar voice. It was Frank, and he wore a smile that was both broad and warm as he joined the group. He slipped an arm around Maggie's waist and kissed the top of her head while keeping his gaze on Stella. She knew they were only recently married, but the love they shared was obvious and made her long to be loved in the way Frank loved his new wife. But her grandmother's words were always with her, pulling her into line, and she knew she had to exercise patience.

She returned his smile. "Thanks, Frank. This looks like a great spread. Thanks for putting it on."

"You're more than welcome. I hope you like steak, because there's plenty of it."

She cringed. Why hadn't she told them? She'd have to now; otherwise it would become too difficult. "Well… I'm…I'm actually vegetarian." She waited for the reaction.

It was slow coming, and the shock was palpable. Finally,

Frank's voice broke the silence. "Vegetarian? How can you be vegetarian and live on a cattle station?"

She shrugged. "I just am. I can't stomach the thought of eating the animals I work on, that's all."

His brows furrowed. "They're not pets."

Maggie looked up at him. "Leave the poor girl alone, Frank. It's okay to be vegetarian."

He wore a glazed expression. "Not where I come from, it's not."

Maggie laughed. "Oh Frank. It's not the end of the world."

"I guess not. But what will you eat?"

Stella perused the tables. "I think there's plenty to choose from. Did you make all these scrumptious dishes?" She asked the question of the three ladies, but Maggie and Olivia quickly deferred to Janella. "Janella's the cook around here," Olivia said, pride in her voice. "She's amazing."

"I can see that. The salads look delicious."

Janella's face lit up, the compliment obviously pleasing her. "Thank you. And now, I think the steaks are ready, so it's time to eat." Her gaze shifted to the barbecue where another man whom Stella guessed might be Olivia's husband was gesturing to her. There was still no sign of Joshua.

Frank cleared his throat and cast his gaze around the group. "Before we give thanks, I'd like to formally welcome Stella to Goddard Downs. Stella, we hope you enjoy living and working here, and we look forward to getting to know you."

She nodded and smiled before he continued. "Now, let's give thanks before we eat." He bowed his head, and in a clear, deep voice, offered a prayer of thanks for the meal, for the family, for the cattle station, and for Stella joining them.

For the next two hours, she enjoyed getting to know the various members of the family, and she shared with them some of her own story, including how, other than the few years she'd lived with her paternal grandmother in Kununurra when she was young and suffered epileptic seizures and needed to be near the hospital, Indigo was the only home she'd known.

Joshua's absence was commented on by everyone, but she noticed that it was Julian who seemed the most annoyed.

CHAPTER 13

*J*oshua sat on a log and nursed the beer he'd been drinking for the past hour. After Stella left, he and Sean finished preparing for the following day's drive. It was a five-nighter, and he wasn't looking forward to it. The group who'd booked it was in for a shock if tonight's party was anything to go by. He doubted some of them would be able to sit in a saddle for an hour, let alone a whole day, or five. And there'd be sore heads tomorrow with the amount of alcohol that was being consumed. His dad and Julian would be furious if they knew what was going on. They'd clearly stipulated from the beginning that the drives were to be alcohol free. That stipulation had deterred some people but pleased others. They hadn't stipulated about the night before the drives began, though. That was a grey area, since most people arrived on the day the drive began. When they arrived the night before, Sean usually offered to host a party, especially if the group comprised single girls, which this one did.

Joshua wasn't in the mood to party. He normally was the one who cooked the burgers and kept an eye on things while Sean mingled, as he called it. But tonight, after he'd finished cooking, Joshua moved to the outskirts and watched from a distance. If they ended up leaving later in the morning, what did it matter? They'd make the first camp easily enough, even if they left at lunchtime. The drives were never overly strenuous, especially on the first day, as he and Sean and the other hands helped the guests with their horses and ensured they were comfortable in the saddle. The second day, when they began driving the steers, was when most of the fun was had. Some guests even tried their hand at roping. Joshua couldn't imagine any of this group having success with that.

The other thing niggling hm was that he'd missed dinner. He couldn't blame Sean for that, although his cousin had continued to make pointed comments about Stella. He considered her a prude and couldn't understand why she didn't want to party. It didn't matter how much Joshua told him that she was entitled to her chosen lifestyle and shouldn't be judged for it, and that perhaps partying wasn't the be all and end all that Sean made it out to be, he continued to put her down, telling Joshua to forget all about her.

But Joshua couldn't. Something about Stella had slid under his skin and wrapped itself around his heart, and despite her faith, she was all he could think of. Today he'd seen a vulnerability in her that he hadn't seen before, and it only made him want to help her get Indigo back, although he had no idea what he could do.

He'd probably wrecked any chance he might have had with her, though. Not turning up for dinner would have put a nail in his coffin. Confirmed he was just like Sean. Good for nothing. He took a final swig of his beer and was about to leave when Sean appeared with a can in one hand and a girl in the other. "What are you doin', cuz? Come and have some fun." He was swaggering and his words were slurred.

Joshua had had enough. "No, mate. I'm going to grab an early night."

"Don't be a party pooper. Here, have this." He shoved the can into Joshua's hand and waved another girl over.

The girl, a blonde who looked to be in her early twenties, sat beside him and began to chat. She was intoxicated, and leaning against him, she slid her hand onto his thigh. "What's the matter, handsome? Don't you want some fun?" She hiccupped and rested her head on his shoulder.

"No, I don't. I'm sorry." He removed her hand.

"Don't you like me?"

"I don't know you. I don't even know your name."

"It's Bree. What's your name?"

"Joshua."

"That's a nice name. What do you do, Joshua?" She hiccupped again.

"I try to keep our guests safe."

"From what?"

"Well, let's see. Safe from falling off their horses after drinking too much. Safe from being chased by feisty steers. Safe from dingoes. Safe from themselves."

"You're a regular life-saver." She giggled.

"I guess you could say that. And right now, I'm going to

keep you safe by telling you to go to bed so you can stay on your horse tomorrow."

"Will you come with me?" Her eyes were large and round as she looked at him.

"Definitely not. I can't make you go, but I strongly suggest you do."

"If that's how it is, I'm going to get another drink." She stumbled when she tried to stand, and if he hadn't reacted quickly and caught her, she would have fallen on top of him. But she used the situation. With a determined hold, she cupped the back of his neck and pulled his mouth against hers and kissed him deeply. Roughly, he flung her away. Bree, whatever her name was, was the last person he wanted to kiss. "Sorry. I'm out of here."

STELLA WAS PREPARING for bed when a sharp knock sounded on her door. Reluctant to open it without knowing who it was, she called out and asked.

"It's Joshua." He didn't sound drunk, but he sounded upset.

Knowing he was on the other side of the door sent her into a spin, but she wasn't overly keen to let him in. "I'll come out. Give me a moment." She quickly slipped out of her pyjamas and into a pair of yoga pants and a loose T-shirt before opening the door.

He stood on the small deck, his hair disheveled and his shirt hanging out of his jeans. Her heart went out to him. "What's wrong, Joshua?"

He shoved his hands in his pockets. "Everything."

"Do you want to talk about it?"

He shrugged. "Maybe. Will you walk with me?"

"In the dark?" Her brows lifted.

"I've got a torch."

Against her better judgment, she agreed. "I'll put my boots on. I don't want to step on a brown snake."

"They'll have shot through with that ruckus going on." He nodded towards the eco tent area where the guests were accommodated.

"Is that where you've been? We missed you at dinner." She sat on the step and pulled her boots on.

"Yeah. Sorry I missed it."

"Did Sean pressure you not to come?"

"Kind of."

She sensed there was another reason he'd skipped dinner but didn't press him. "Okay, lead the way. I don't think we need the torch," she said as he led them in the opposite direction from the party she could now hear. Moonlight beamed down on them, lighting up the track. They walked in silence for several minutes. Stella snatched a few glances of him, and each time, her heart lurched. Perhaps it was her nurturing nature that made her want to give him a hug and tell him everything would be okay, but it was more than that. She was extremely conscious of his masculinity, and his nearness kindled feelings in her she didn't want. But that wasn't quite true. She *did* want to experience such feelings one day, but she was cautious of going against her grandmother's advice and allowing herself to embrace them now.

She put a little distance between them and asked what was bothering him.

He sighed heavily and raked a hand through his already messed up hair. "I'm tired of getting shoved around by everyone and not getting a say in what I do."

"Really? Who else tries to control you, other than Sean?"

"My brother."

"Julian?"

"Yep."

"I don't have any siblings, but I'm fairly sure it's normal for siblings to jostle with each other." She was going to add, especially when they're both drop-dead handsome, but stopped herself just in time.

"He's a jerk."

"I met him tonight. He actually seemed really nice."

"You don't know him."

"Maybe the two of you are too similar."

"Are you calling me a jerk as well?"

She winced. "I didn't mean that. I meant that you're both strong personalities, and that perhaps you're both fighting to be the top dog."

"I gave that dream up long ago."

"Did you?"

He shrugged. "Maybe not. Maybe I just don't know what I want."

"Do you really want to leave Goddard Downs?"

He looked at her and her heart lurched again. Even in the half-light, his eyes were mesmerising. "I don't know."

They stopped when they reached an outlook. "Do you want to sit?" he asked.

"Okay," she replied.

He found a flat rock and waited for her to sit before joining her. It would be so easy to rest her head against his shoulder. She imagined his arm around her but quickly pulled herself up. Thoughts like that would only lead to confusion and heartache. She said she'd be his friend, and that's what she'd be. Nothing more, nothing less.

"You're different when you're not with Sean."

"You think so?"

"Yes. I don't like talking ill of people, but he's not a great influence."

He sighed heavily. "I guess I know that, but he's the only friend I have."

"You have me."

His gaze lifted to hers, and for a moment she thought he would kiss her. A shaky breath quivered out of her as he lifted his hand and gently caressed the side of her cheek.

"Stella..." In slow motion, he bent towards her. Her gaze was drawn to his mouth, and she could almost taste his lips. But no. She couldn't allow this to happen.

"I'm sorry, Joshua. We can't do this." As she moved her head away, she saw the disappointment in his eyes, but there was nothing she could do. Nothing she could live with, anyway.

"Why, Stella? Why can't we be more than friends? Please tell me."

She couldn't tell him the entire reason, but she could offer hope of something more once they knew each other better.

He seemed to accept that, and he even opened up further about how he felt about Julian. She could see it wasn't just a simple sibling spat. It was a deep seated, ongoing feud that could very easily result in Joshua leaving Goddard Downs for good. And that was the last thing she wanted.

After a while, they strolled back. When they reached the staff accommodation block, he faced her, and looking deep into her eyes, asked if he could hug her.

Against her better judgment, she said yes. As his strong arms encircled her and she felt the warmth of his body against hers, her heart picked up its pace. She slipped her arms around his waist and rested her head in the hollow between his shoulder and neck.

With a gentle kiss to her head, he exhaled and released his hold. "Thank you."

She smiled. "Thank *you*."

Their gazes met and held and despite her resolve, she knew she was falling in love.

"I hope Brutus behaves for you tomorrow. I won't be back for a few days, so I won't hear about it until then."

"I'm sure I'll be fine. And I hope the drive goes well."

"Thanks. I somehow doubt it will, but I might be surprised."

"I'll be praying for you."

"Thanks." He smiled before turning and walking away.

She took some deep, slow breaths and sent up a prayer, not just for him, but for herself. She was in unchartered waters, and more than anything, she needed God's direction, because the last thing she wanted was to make a mistake.

CHAPTER 14

*T*aking a sip of his tea, Frank rested his elbows on the railing and gazed across the paddocks to the mountain ranges in the distance. Caleb was beside him, but instead of sipping on tea, his grandson was nursing a Coke. The pair were taking a mid-morning break while doing some final touch-ups on the old Jeep Caleb had been given as a thirteenth birthday present. Frank treasured the time spent with his grandson. All too soon, Caleb would be at boarding school in Darwin, and although he'd be home during the holidays, he would come back changed. Not that change was a bad thing. Being at boarding school would give Caleb opportunities he'd never get at the station. But Caleb didn't want to go. With their heads under the bonnet and their hands covered in grease, Frank had been regaling him with stories of his own time at boarding school in an attempt to encourage him.

"I met your grandmother at school," he said after taking

another sip of tea, his gaze fixed on a wedge-tailed eagle soaring high in the deep blue sky.

"Yeah, I know. You've told me that like a hundred times."

Frank faced him and chuckled. "I dare say I have. I'm sorry. It's just that I have such fond memories of my time at school, and I'm excited for you, son. You'll make lifelong friends while you're there, and it'll do you good to mix with boys your own age instead of hanging out with your old grandfather."

"But I like hanging out with you."

Frank smiled. "That's very kind of you to say that, but you don't know what you're missing out on."

"I guess so. It's just scary, that's all."

"I know. We've all felt that way, but you'll soon settle in. And besides, you've still got almost half a year before you go." Frank took a final sip of his tea and set his mug on the table. "Anyway, if you want to drive this Jeep before you go, we'd best get back to it."

"How much longer is it going to take?"

"Oh, I'm not sure, but I'm guessing we might get it running today."

Caleb's eyes enlarged. "Really?"

"Yep. We'll do a final tune-up and then it should be good to go."

"Will you teach me to drive? Dad said he would, but he's busy all the time."

"So long as he's okay with that, I'd love to." Frank ruffled Caleb's hair and smiled. He'd stepped into the project after Julian had taken over the management role at the station, giving Frank more time to not only spend with Maggie, but to do things like this. It had been a trade-off for Julian, but Frank was pleased that Julian had at least done most of the work with Caleb, forging a better relationship with his son.

As they were about to head back to the Jeep, Joshua pulled up outside the shed in a truck and jumped out.

"Have you come to help?" Caleb asked as Joshua hurried inside.

"Sorry. I've just come to pick up some drinks for tomorrow's drive. How's it coming along?"

"Grandpa said it should be done today."

"Great." There was something about Joshua's tone that pricked Frank's conscience. He still hadn't had that talk with his son, but he needed to.

"Caleb, can you get a rag and start cleaning the grease off the metal work while I have a quick chat with Uncle Josh?"

"Sure."

Frank followed Joshua out and rested a hand against the truck while Joshua loaded it. "So, son, how is everything? It's been a while since we caught up."

Joshua shrugged. "Nothing's changed."

"Things still rough with Julian?"

"Yeah." He let out a heavy sigh. "I'm not sure why he's got it in for me."

"It beats me, too. I'll have another word with him."

"It won't do any good."

"There's no harm in trying. It grieves me to see my two grown sons at each other all the time."

"I just try to avoid him."

"I guess that's not too hard with so many drives booked."

"Yeah." Joshua heaved another crate onto the bed of the

truck and then lifted his hat off and wiped his brow with the back of his hand.

"I'd like to catch up properly one day soon. Do you think you and I could head out for an overnighter later this week?" Frank asked.

"Feeling guilty, are we?"

Frank narrowed his eyes. "No, son. I'd just like to spend some time with you before Maggie and I head off to Darwin next week. Anything wrong with that?"

"Guess not. I'll see what I can fit in."

"Good. Let me know."

Joshua jumped into the truck and tipped his hat before driving off, leaving Frank with the distinct feeling that his son was at a crossroads in his life. Although Frank had convinced him to stay at Goddard Downs for the rest of the season, he sensed that Joshua's emotions were like a smouldering fire that could reignite at the drop of a hat.

MAGGIE WAS in the vegetable patch and had a clear line of sight to the shed where Frank and Caleb were working on the old Jeep. She was crouched down while she tended to the vegetables, so Frank hadn't seen her, but she'd seen Joshua stop by and she prayed that Frank was able to talk with him about the issues between him and Julian. With Joshua so busy with the drives, it hadn't been easy for the pair to catch up.

As Joshua drove off in the truck, her phone rang. She already knew it was Serena from the ringtone. Quickly removing her gloves, she pulled the phone from her pocket and answered it. "Serena, how are you are?"

"It's started. The baby's coming." She was panting already, although Maggie guessed it was more from emotion than from pain. Nevertheless, Maggie's pulse sped up.

"It's too early, darling."

"I know, but the doctor said it will be okay."

"Alright. I'll get Frank and we'll come now. But it'll take us at least twelve hours to get there."

"I know. I'm sorry, Mum. You didn't plan on coming until next week."

"It's okay. We're not doing anything that's more important than being with you."

"I'm scared, Mum." Her voice faltered and Maggie's heart went out to her.

"You'll be fine, sweetheart. David's with you, isn't he?"

"Yes."

"And we'll be praying for you."

"Thank you. I've got to go."

"Okay. We'll get updates from David when we can, and we'll be there as soon as possible."

"Thank you."

Slipping her phone back into her pocket, Maggie hurried to the shed and conveyed the news to Frank. Although he said the right words, she sensed he wasn't overly happy about the timing.

CHAPTER 15

The drive to Darwin seemed to take forever. After Maggie told Frank the news, he'd quickly cleaned himself up and told Caleb the Jeep would have to wait, unless his dad could find the time to finish it with him. Caleb tried to hide his disappointment, but his dropped shoulders gave it away. Maggie felt bad. She hated disappointing the boy, but she needed to be there for her daughter. After all Serena had been through, she prayed that bringing a new life into the world would be the final step in Serena's journey back to wholeness. Not that her external scars would ever completely disappear, but she was growing in her faith and regaining her confidence, and that was what mattered the most. Serena, however, did worry what her child would think of her when he was old enough to know she didn't look like everyone else. Maggie had assured her that he would love her just the same.

They arrived in Darwin just before midnight and headed straight for the hospital. David had told them that Serena was doing well and was fully dilated. The baby should be coming soon. On the phone, he'd sounded anxious, which was to be expected. Face to face, he seemed calmer, and greeted them both with a hug. "Thanks for coming so quickly."

Maggie chuckled. "I wouldn't miss this for the world. I'm just glad we got here before the baby. Can we see Serena?"

"Yes, I told the midwife you were coming, and she said it's fine. Serena's not in the labour ward yet but will be soon."

"Great. I can't wait to see her." Maggie slipped her arm into the crook of Frank's elbow for support. She couldn't remember being quite so emotional when her other two grandchildren were born, but perhaps she had been.

They followed David through the ward until they reached Serena's room. Maggie heard her before she saw her and her heart clenched. Although it had been years since she herself had given birth, she could still remember the pain. But she also knew it was short lived and as soon as Serena held her child in her arms, it would be forgotten. At thirty-six weeks, the baby might need to go into an incubator for a time. All these thoughts flooded Maggie's mind before she entered the room, but as soon as she saw Serena lying in the bed, she couldn't stop tears from flowing as emotion welled inside her. She left Frank's side and rushed over and gave Serena a big hug. "Oh darling, how are you doing?"

Serena shuffled up in the bed and hugged her back. "It hurts so much."

"I know, but it'll be over soon." Maggie straightened and brushed Serena's brow. It amazed her that she no longer noticed Serena's distorted skin. It seemed normal now.

Serena nodded. "I hope so."

Maggie squeezed her hand. "Is there anything we can get you?"

"Drugs."

Maggie laughed. "I think you'll need to ask the nurse for those."

"I already have. She said I don't need any yet."

"You must be doing well, then." Maggie glanced at David and he nodded.

"I just want the baby to come."

"I know you do. By the look of you, it won't be much longer."

"I hope not." She doubled over in pain and moaned.

David rubbed her back while Maggie squeezed her hand. "You can do this, darling. Short breaths."

The contraction passed and the midwife entered. After a quick examination, she said it was time to go to the labour ward. Maggie gave Serena another hug and promised to pray for her. She then hugged David and leaned against Frank as Serena was wheeled away.

Left alone, they headed back to the waiting room. Only two others were there, a woman who looked to be in her fifties, and a younger woman Maggie guessed was her daughter since they shared similar facial features. Maggie smiled and asked if they were waiting for a baby. The older woman said yes, her daughter was in labour. Maggie told her that she and Frank were also waiting. She sat beside him and wondered how long they'd have to wait. For Serena's sake, she prayed it wouldn't be long.

After two hours with no news, Maggie started to worry. Frank placed his hand over hers and assured her that Serena was fine.

"How do you know? We haven't heard anything for hours."
Her voice was elevated. She took some slow breaths. "I'm
sorry. You're right. I think I'm tired and not thinking straight."

"It's been a long day."

She rested her head on his shoulder. "I'm sorry for taking
you away from Caleb, and for making you delay your getaway
with Joshua."

"I'm sure they'll survive."

"Yes, but the timing wasn't great, was it?"

He chuckled. "There was nothing we could do about that,
my love. Babies make an appearance in their own time, and
only God knows when that is."

Moments later, David burst through the double doors with
a broad grin on his face.

Frank chuckled. "I guess that time has just come."

Maggie jumped up and peered into her son-in-law's eyes.
"Looks like everything's okay?"

"Yes, we have a healthy son. He's small but the doctor said
he's fighting fit."

Tears pricked Maggie's eyes as she threw her arms around
him. "Just like his father. Congratulations."

David chuckled. "Thank you. But I don't think his father's
so fighting fit these days." After Maggie released him, he asked
if she and Frank would like to see the baby.

"Of course we do. Lead the way."

Maggie clung to Frank as they followed David to the
neonatal ward. They were instructed to put on gowns and
masks to minimise the risk of infection. Once ready, they
tiptoed into the cubicle where Serena lay in a bed holding

the tiny baby boy in her arms. She looked up, her face beaming.

Maggie couldn't stem the flow of tears as she stepped closer and kissed the top of Serena's head before inspecting the baby, whom they'd named Oliver. He was perfect. All her fears were forgotten as Serena carefully handed him to her and she cradled him in her arms. "Hello, little Oliver. Welcome to our family."

The little boy cooed, and she knew she was imagining it, but it seemed his gaze was fixed on her. She showed him to Frank and then handed him back to Serena. "He's beautiful, darling. Congratulations."

"Thanks, Mum. I think I'm in heaven. It was so amazing."

"I told you you'd be fine."

"I should have listened." Serena chuckled and then kissed the top of her son's head.

"I think we'll head off and grab some sleep if you don't mind," Maggie said, stifling a yawn.

"Not at all. My keys are somewhere." Serena looked on either side of her before David pulled a set from his pocket and handed them to Frank. "Excuse the mess. We didn't plan for this to happen today, but the spare bed is made up. Make yourself at home."

"Thanks," Frank said, slapping him lightly on the back. "We'll be just fine."

"Good. I'm not sure when I'll get home."

"There's no hurry. Stay as long as you want, although you'll both probably need some sleep soon."

"I don't know that I'd sleep at the moment," David said, turning his gaze to Serena and Oliver.

"Well, we'll see you when we see you. We'll come back once we've had a rest. Is there anything we can get you?"

"A beer..."

Frank chuckled. "I'm not sure they allow it in here, but I can check."

"Don't worry. I was only joking." David chuckled along with him.

"Okay then, we'll leave you for now. Congratulations once again." Frank smiled at the trio and then slipped his arm around Maggie's waist. "Come on, my love, let's get some shut eye."

"Sounds good to me. See you soon." She smiled and waved to the little family before leaving them and heading down the corridor towards the car park.

Although it was still dark, the horizon was light, heralding the dawn of a new day. Maggie leaned against Frank and hummed one of her favourite worship songs as her heart filled with gratitude for a safe delivery and the birth of a precious baby boy:

The steadfast love of the Lord never ceases
His mercies never come to an end
They are new every morning
New every morning
Great is Thy faithfulness, O Lord
Great is Thy faithfulness

CHAPTER 16

Stella was working in the stables when Joshua walked in carrying two saddles. She guessed he hadn't seen her since she was crouched down in a stall attending to one of the cows who'd recently given birth but had developed mastitis. She'd already administered the medication and was now gently hand milking the cow to relieve the pressure on her swollen teat. The poor cow was letting out a moan every now and then, so Stella tried to be as gentle as possible. While she milked, she kept her gaze on Joshua, who'd thrown the saddles onto the work bench and was now giving them a thorough cleaning.

It was difficult to watch him and retain a regular rhythm on the infected teat. He was close enough for her to see the stubble on his face and the honed muscles that filled out his shirt as he rubbed the saddles.

Over the past two weeks, she'd seen him on and off between drives, but had intentionally avoided being alone with him. It wasn't that she didn't trust him; she didn't trust herself. She was growing fonder of him every day, but she wasn't ready to take the next step and move from friendship to something more. She didn't know when that time would come, although she prayed about it every day. His lack of faith concerned her, although she sensed that he still believed. He was simply angry with the world, and probably with God. She'd seen how patient he was with the guests, and how he played with his nephews and nieces when he was home. He'd even finished the Jeep with Caleb after Frank had left unexpectedly and taken him for driving lessons along the tracks that wound through the property when he could.

It was only when Joshua was near Julian and Sean that his other side came out. It was strange, because she'd found Julian to be a good boss. After she'd successfully inoculated Brutus and given him his annual checkup without incident, Julian's opinion of her seemed to have improved. She was starting to feel like she'd been accepted, although she kept reminding herself that this job was a means to an end. The end was getting Indigo back. The bank had put the station on the market, but as far as she knew, there weren't any buyers. Yet. She prayed there wouldn't be. She hadn't disclosed her intentions to her parents, as she wanted to surprise them. The last thing she wanted was to disappoint them if she failed in her quest. She'd been ignoring the possibility of failing, but in her quiet times, that verse hounded her. *Seek first the Kingdom of God, and all these things will be added unto you.* She assured God in her prayer time that she *was* seeking Him first. That nothing stood between Him and her. Sometimes she wondered if she was simply trying to convince herself of that, because she seemed unable to ask Him to search her heart, to see if there was any wicked way in her. If she was indeed seeking Him first.

Joshua glanced up and their gazes met. Her cheeks warmed at being caught studying him. His smile was alluring, the kind that made her insides turn to flame. "I didn't know you were there." His voice held a trace of laughter.

"Sorry. I've been tending this sick cow. She's got mastitis and I've been milking her infected teat."

He made a face. "Sounds painful."

Stella did one last squirt then straightened. "Yes, poor thing." She patted the cow and carried the bucket of milk to the tub where she emptied it out before disinfecting the bucket. "How are you doing?"

"Not bad."

"But not good, either?"

"I didn't say that."

"You didn't have to." She gave him a pointed look.

"Okay." He ran a hand across his head. "Not good, either."

She leaned back against the tub and folded her arms. "What's wrong?"

"The usual."

Stella groaned. She was growing tired of Joshua's constant complaining about his brother. She honestly couldn't see what the problem was, apart from them both having a little too much testosterone. She gulped. Make that a lot of extra testosterone in Joshua's case. Why did he have to look so hot as he rubbed that saddle?

"Would you like to have lunch with me?"

The question came out of the blue and her brows scrunched. "What? At the homestead?"

"No. I made sangas. I was planning on riding out to the ridge and eating them there. Get away from everyone. I've got enough for you."

"I bet they have meat on them."

"They do, but I can take it off."

She chuckled as she rolled her eyes. "The taste would still be there."

"I'll make some new ones. Why don't you like meat? I don't get it."

She shrugged. "I never have. I don't like the taste and I prefer vegetables."

"Simple as that, huh?"

"Yes."

"Crazy."

"What did you say?" Sidling up to him, she crossed her arms and waited for an answer.

He stuttered before he said, "Daisy. Is that the name of the cow?"

She burst out laughing. "You're not a good liar."

He shrugged and his eyes twinkled, and for a moment their gazes were locked. He cleared his throat. "Anyway, what do you say about lunch?"

"Okay, it's a deal. But I'll make my own sandwiches."

"You don't trust me?"

"No."

"Well, that says it all, doesn't it?"

"I guess so." She grinned. "What time do you want to go?" She checked her watch. It was almost midday.

"A bit after twelve?"

"That works for me. I'll go and make my sandwiches. I gather we're riding."

"Yes. I can bring Amber to your place if you like."

"Sounds good. See you then."

"See ya."

After leaving the shed, she expelled a huge breath. But she also wore the widest of grins.

JOSHUA QUICKLY FINISHED CLEANING the saddles and prepared the horses. He had his sandwiches with him, so as soon as he was ready, he mounted Flame and led Amber to Stella's unit. She was coming out the door when he arrived.

"That was good timing." Her smile lit up her face and he couldn't help but think how gorgeous she was. She was wearing khaki shorts and a shirt, her normal work attire, and on anyone else, the outfit would look drab, but on her, it looked amazing. Although she was tall, her legs were shapely and tanned, and she had muscles in her arms that spoke of hard work. Since she'd been at Goddard Downs, he'd seen how much effort she put into her work. She was a trooper, that was for sure, and he could see himself settling down with her. If only she wanted that too. She'd started to relax with him, and that gave him hope.

She mounted Amber easily, and they set off. The ridge wasn't far, so they took it slowly. The next drive was two days away, so for once, he wasn't in a hurry. They chatted about what animals she'd been looking after, and the last drive he'd been on. Neither felt compelled to fill in the short periods of silence. They simply enjoyed the ride and each other's company. To Joshua, being with Stella felt right, and he was contemplating telling Sean he wouldn't be leaving with him at the end of the season. Sean wouldn't be happy, but Joshua had been growing weary of his cousin's wild ways. If it wasn't for Julian, he'd be more than happy to stay at Goddard Downs over the wet season and beyond, if Stella was still there.

They arrived at the ridge, and after dismounting, they tethered the horses to a tree. He cleared a patch of earth and threw a blanket down, apologising for its tattiness. He carried it in his saddle bag and used it only occasionally. He should have washed it, but he hadn't planned on sharing it with Stella. She said it was fine and when she sat down, she stretched her legs in front of her. He drank in the nearness of her. Each time he saw her, the pull was stronger and he longed to hold her. To kiss her. But he knew he had to be patient or else he'd push her away. She wanted their relationship to develop slowly, and for them to get to know each other before they went any further, so that's what they had to do, whether he liked it or not.

Opening his lunch bag, he pulled out his sandwiches. Roast beef and mustard on rye. Nothing better. He looked at hers and turned up his nose. "Salad? Is that all you've got?"

"What's wrong with that?"

"Nothing, I guess, if you're a cow."

"Are you calling me a cow?"

"I wouldn't dare."

"You'd better not!" She laughed and he relaxed. As they ate, they gazed out at the breathtaking vista. The rich ochre of the rock-faced mountains contrasted with the deep blue of the sky that stretched forever. Several kites soared above the savannah scrubland dotted with termite mounds, seeking out small prey to swoop down on and devour. Joshua much preferred eating his lunch away from the homestead when he could. Not only was it peaceful here, there was no chance of an argument starting with Julian.

"There's a ridge like this on Indigo," Stella said matter-of-factly, but there was a wistful tone in her voice.

"You miss it, don't you?"

She faced him and nodded. "I sure do. It's home."

"Well, I hope you get it back."

"So do I."

"Is Indigo the only place you've ever lived?"

"Yes, apart from a few years when I lived with my grand-mother in Kununurra when I was in and out of hospital, and the years I spent at university."

"Which one did you go to?"

"Murdoch Uni in Perth."

"Your parents must have been proud of you."

"They weren't keen on me going to uni. They just wanted me to work on the station, but being a vet was all I ever wanted to do, so I paid my own way."

"Wow. That's dedication."

"It helps when you're passionate about something."

"I guess so."

"What about you?" She leaned back on her elbows. "Did you ever want to study after you left school?"

"No. I went on the circuit as soon as I could."

"How did your dad feel about that?"

"He wasn't happy. Said he hadn't spent all that money on boarding school to have me become a bull rider."

"What made you want to do it?"

He shrugged. "I didn't feel there was a place for me here."

"I'm sure that wasn't true."

"Maybe. But that's how I felt. It would have been different if Mum had still been around."

"You must miss her."

"Yep. Everything would be different if she were here."

"You mean with Julian?"

He nodded.

"God can heal riffs."

"He'd have a hard time healing this one. Julian's a jerk to the nth degree."

"In your opinion."

He narrowed his eyes. "Do you like him?"

"I don't dislike him. I've found him to be quite reasonable."

"You must be talking about a different person."

"No. I'm talking about Julian Goddard. Your brother."

"He must be putting on a show for you."

"Maybe, but I don't get that impression. I think it's that the two of you are trying to prove something to each other. That's my observation, anyway."

"Whatever. Can we not talk about him?"

"Okay. What do you want to talk about?"

He wanted to say 'us', but he stopped himself and instead replied, "What about you. Tell me about you."

She shrugged. "There's nothing much to say."

He quirked a brow. "I don't think that's true."

STELLA INHALED DEEPLY. Joshua was right. There was actually a lot she could say about herself. She could tell him about the months she'd spent in the hospital as a child, her epileptic seizures, living with her grandmother, being separated from her parents, meeting the Lord as a young girl, and what her uni years were like. But they didn't have all day, so she had to choose, or give him the truckload in a nutshell.

She decided to tell him about the day she gave her heart to the Lord, because out of everything, that was the most important moment in her life.

"I was ten when I gave my heart to the Lord."

"Ten? That's young."

She nodded. "I guess so, but I knew what I was doing. It was while I was living with my grandmother. Mum and Dad couldn't leave Indigo, but I needed to be near the hospital because of my seizures, so my grandmother invited me to live with her. She was an amazing woman, generous and kind to everyone. My grandfather died in a road accident when she was forty. I never knew him, but from the way she talked about him, they loved each other a lot. She never remarried. She said she'd been blessed to have one true love in her life, and she was more than satisfied with that. Plus, she had her faith. She used to take me to church on Sundays, and afterwards we'd go to the park and eat lunch while we talked about what I'd learned in Sunday school. Between my Sunday school lessons and Gran, I think I learned all the Bible stories inside and out."

"What was your favourite?"

"That's a hard one, but I think Daniel in the lion's den. Each time I had a seizure I thought I was going to die, and each time, I thought of Daniel and how brave he was, and how much he trusted God to save him. I called out to God and asked Him to do the same for me. He did. I could have died at least one of those times, but I didn't. I know some people are skeptical when they hear that, but He was so real to me in my time of need, and after the third time, I asked Jesus into my heart. Gran explained how God had sent His only Son to earth as a perfect human to take on my sin by dying on the cross so that I could stand clean before God. I got baptised in the river down by the church the week after, and ever since, I've been living for Him."

"That was more than I bargained for."

"Sorry. But you asked me to tell you about myself, and my faith is the most important thing in my life, so it made sense to tell you about how it came about."

"More important than getting Indigo back?"

There it was again, that niggling question. Of course her faith was more important than a cattle station. *But was it?*

"Of course. My faith is everything. So, I've told you about me. Now it's your turn."

He glanced at his watch. "Out of time, sorry. I've got to get back."

"Thought you said you weren't on a schedule today."

"I just remembered some things I've got to do."

She didn't believe him for one moment, but he obviously wasn't ready to open up about himself, so she wouldn't push him. There'd be another time, of that she was sure. In the meantime, she'd pray that his heart would open to God, who not only knew everything about him, but loved him in spite of it.

They packed up their picnic and rode the horses back. Neither spoke much, as she was lost in thought and it seemed he was, too. Arriving back at the stables, they got off the horses and tethered them to the rail. Having not been worked hard, they didn't need grooming. Stella had animals to attend to, so she thanked Joshua for sharing his lunch break with her and turned to leave, but he called her back.

"Thanks for sharing all that." Their gazes met and held. Her heart picked up its pace as his clear blue eyes pierced the distance between them.

She could have so easily walked back to him. Wrapped her arms around him. Kissed him. But that would be going against her resolve and what she believed was right. Instead, she smiled and said, "You're welcome," before turning and walking away.

CHAPTER 17

*T*hree days later, Stella was still trying to ignore Joshua's question about whether her faith was more important to her than getting Indigo back.

She threw herself into her work and focused on the animals in her care. And there were plenty of them. The deal with the Indonesian buyer had gone through and a new load of cattle had just arrived. Each animal needed to be thoroughly checked before being released from the holding paddock to reduce the risk of any disease spreading to the healthy stock. It was demanding work, but having assured Frank and Julian she was equal to the challenge, she had no choice but to work from dawn to dusk. The benefit was that it kept her thoughts from wandering. As soon as her head hit the pillow at night, she was asleep.

One more day and she'd be finished, and then she had two days off. Her cousin, Elizabeth, was coming to visit from Kununurra, and Stella was looking forward to seeing her.

Although she loved Goddard Downs, she missed her family. She talked to her parents every other night, and occasionally zoomed with them, but the internet reception was erratic and it didn't work overly well. Each time she spoke with them, she struggled to stay positive. Her parents had been on a downward spiral since losing Indigo, and everything they said was negative. Other than getting the station back and praying for them, Stella didn't know how to help them. She often wondered why her dad, in particular, had never made a commitment to the Lord, especially because his mother, Stella's grandmother, was so committed.

Her grandmother had prayed for him and Stella's mum every day, firmly believing that God would answer her prayers and bring them both to salvation, but she'd died without seeing her prayers answered. She'd passed the baton to Stella as she slipped into the Lord's arms, and so Stella felt the burden of responsibility for them. Not that it was a burden, really. She longed for her parents to find peace and purpose, and to understand that God truly did love them and hadn't taken Indigo from them out of spite. She'd come to accept that it had been a combination of her dad's poor management skills and him not seeking help, along with the live cattle export ban, that had caused their demise. She knew he blamed himself, along with God, and not only did she worry about the state of his spiritual health, but she also worried about his mental health. As much as she didn't like to admit it, he was a high suicide risk, and she prayed daily that he would seek help before it was too late.

Straightening, she stretched and surveyed the remaining cattle. The line was dwindling, which was good, because her back was starting to ache. She called to Tommo, the hand who was moving the cattle around for her, and asked him to bring the next couple of steers into the stalls. They were good looking animals, and she was sure they'd do well and fetch a good price once fully grown. She couldn't help but compare how well managed Goddard Downs was compared to Indigo. She longed for the opportunity to rebuild it, but although her bank balance was growing now she was employed, it was a far cry from what she needed. As the steers entered the stalls, she asked the Lord to find a way to get it back.

Three hours later, Stella was driving back from the holding pens when she noticed a cloud of red dust hovering in the air along the track leading to the homestead. Looking at her watch, she guessed it was Elizabeth, so instead of returning to her unit, she drove in the other direction to meet her. They arrived at the intersecting crossroads at the same time, and after pulling their vehicles to the side, they jumped out and hugged each other.

"Hey, girl. How are you doing?" Elizabeth peered into Stella's eyes as she asked the question. Two years younger, she was slightly shorter and had dark curly hair that framed her round face. She'd inherited her mother's olive skin, broad nose, and warm, brown eyes which came from her indigenous heritage. Nobody would think that Stella and Elizabeth were related, but not only were they good friends, they were first cousins. Elizabeth had trained as a nurse and helped care for their grandmother as she ailed.

"Great. How about you?" Smiling at her cousin, Stella forgot about her tired, sore back.

"Much better now I'm here. That drive was a doozy."

"I know. But it's worth it, you'll see. It's lovely here."

Elizabeth shooed the flies buzzing around her face and nodded. "It sure is. You've landed on your feet here."

"I have. I'll give you a tour, but let's freshen up first. I've been working with cattle all day and I think I smell."

"I wondered what it was." Elizabeth sniffed the air.

Stella laughed. "Come on. Follow me. My unit's just down here."

"Right you are."

They climbed into their vehicles. Elizabeth was driving an old Suzuki Jimny she'd had for years. Stella had encouraged her to trade it in and get a newer vehicle, but Elizabeth said she loved her Suzi and wouldn't part with it until it died. Stella hoped that wouldn't happen on this trip.

She led the way to the staff accommodation area and parked under the shade of the gum trees. Elizabeth pulled her Suzi up beside her and after climbing out, followed her inside. She dropped her bags and inspected the unit. "This is neat, Stell. I'll take the couch."

"No, you won't. You're my guest, so you'll have my bed and I'll sleep out here. The couch is a pull-out, and I'll be fine."

Elizabeth shrugged. "I won't argue with you. But you take the first shower. I insist on that."

Stella laughed again. "I get the message. Okay, I won't be long. Make yourself at home. There are cold drinks in the fridge, or have a hot drink if you prefer."

"Thanks. I'll be alright."

Smiling, Stella grabbed a fresh change of clothes and headed to the bathroom. The warm water felt so good and she was tempted to stay longer, but Elizabeth was waiting, so she quickly washed herself, and once dry, slipped into her white capris and a sleeveless, light-blue T. She pulled her hair into a ponytail and emerged to find that Elizabeth had prepared what looked to be an entire feast.

"Wow. You brought all this with you?" She'd prepared a grazing platter loaded with crackers and breadsticks, a variety of cheeses, black and green olives, dried tomatoes, and home-made avocado dip. There was no meat on the platter, but there was a side dish that held some salami slices.

Elizabeth grinned. "I thought you could do with some spoiling."

Tears pricked Stella's eyes as she smiled gratefully. "Thank you. This is amazing. Let's go out onto the deck and have it there. You don't want to freshen up first?"

"No, I'm fine. I've only been driving."

"Okay. So, what do you want to drink?"

"I brought some non-alcoholic cider. I wasn't sure you'd have any left."

"You thought of everything!" Elizabeth was right. Stella's supplies of her favourite drink had run out a few days earlier.

"I hope so." Elizabeth grabbed two cans from her cooler bag and followed Stella onto the small deck. Stella carried the platter and placed it onto the round table before sitting on one of the metal chairs.

"This is really nice," Elizabeth said as she popped the lid on her can and took a sip.

"The cider or the setting?"

"The setting, silly!"

Stella laughed, and easing back in the chair, took a sip of her own drink. "It's really peaceful out here."

"But?"

Stella's brows furrowed. "But what?"

"I hear longing in your voice."

Stella groaned inwardly. Why did Elizabeth have to be so perceptive?

"You'd rather be at Indigo?" Elizabeth looked at her pointedly.

Stella drew a breath and released it slowly. "Yes."

"You have to let it go, Stell. God must have better plans for you."

"You sound like Gran."

"I take that as a compliment."

"I still miss her." Stella put her drink on the floor beside her and cut some camembert and placed it on a cracker.

"I do, too. She was a special woman. And she would have told you that when God closes a door, He usually opens another. Talking of that, how's it been going with Joshua?" Elizabeth raised a thick, dark eyebrow, an expectant expression on her face.

Stella had been dreading that question. Elizabeth hadn't met him, but she'd heard about him. Stella had made the mistake of telling her cousin about the handsome cowboy she'd danced with at the rodeo in Alice, and Elizabeth had wheedled out of her more information than she'd planned on disclosing. She needed to be cautious in her reply or else she'd never hear the end of it. "We're friends."

Elizabeth's brow lifted further. "Friends?"

Stella nodded.

"Is that all?"

"Yes."

"I'm not sure I believe you. You'll have to introduce us, and then I'll be able to see for myself if you're telling the truth or not."

That's what concerned Stella, but there was little she could do about it. They probably couldn't avoid seeing him at some stage over the next two days since he wasn't away on a drive. "If we see him, I will. He stays away from the homestead as much as he can."

"Well, I'll look forward to meeting him."

Stella gave a smile that she knew didn't quite meet her eyes.

A short while later, after they'd devoured the platter, Stella offered to give Elizabeth a quick tour of the property. "Just the section near the homestead this afternoon since it's getting late. We can explore more tomorrow."

"Sounds good to me."

They set off in Stella's Jeep since Elizabeth was a town girl and not overly comfortable in the saddle, despite Stella's attempts to teach her to ride. She headed the Jeep up the track she and Joshua had ridden on her first day at Goddard Downs. It was bumpy and she had to navigate a few deep ruts, but the Jeep handled it easily. She stopped and pointed out some of the new cattle she'd been attending to. The ones that concerned her enough to keep in the fenced paddock near the homestead where she could keep an eye on them before allowing them to mix with the rest of the herd.

"You haven't been on one of the drives?" Elizabeth asked as she looked across the paddock.

"No. They're for paying guests."

"I thought Joshua might have invited you to tag along on one."

Stella flashed her a steely-eyed look. "How could I take time off when I've just started a new job?"

Elizabeth shrugged and then continued on. Reaching the top, Stella brought the Jeep to a halt and the pair climbed out to enjoy the view. It was late afternoon, and the sun, low in the sky, bathed the savannah plains in a golden haze. They enjoyed the vista for ten minutes before Stella suggested they head back before it got dark.

A short while later, as she drove by the big work shed, she realised she'd made a mistake going that way. Joshua and Sean were outside tying a load onto the truck they used for the drives. Joshua tipped his hat and caught Stella's gaze. She felt her cheeks flush. She gave a quick nod and intended to drive on when Elizabeth said, "Is that him? What a hunk. You've got to stop and introduce us."

Against her better judgment, Stella slowed the Jeep and brought it to a halt.

SINCE THEIR PICNIC lunch two days earlier, Joshua had seen little of Stella. She'd been tied up with the new cattle, and he and Sean were doing a thorough clean of the shed. He'd bristled when Julian dished out the job. He might be the manager, but his brother hadn't stepped foot in the shed in years as far as Joshua knew. Julian simply took delight in lording it over Joshua whenever he could. With the next drive two days away, he and Sean had already intended to clean it out, but now they were doing it begrudgingly.

Seeing Stella, his mood suddenly buoyed. A smile tipped his

lips when she stopped her Jeep and got out. Wearing figure-hugging capris and a blue sleeveless T-shirt, she looked fresh and gorgeous. Another woman got out. Shorter, darker, plumper, but with a jolly face and a wide grin as she walked towards him holding her hand out. "You must be Joshua."

He blinked and glanced at Stella before nodding and shaking the other woman's hand. "Yes, and you are?"

"Elizabeth, Stella's cousin."

"Right." That meant Stella had talked about him. That was good. And by the grin her cousin wore, it seemed that what she'd said was favourable.

"I'm visiting for a couple of days and she's just taken me on a quick tour. It's a great property."

"Glad you like it."

Her gaze shifted to Sean who was standing to the side, arms folded, taking in the scene with a smirk on his face. "And you must be Sean," she added.

He stepped forward and shook her hand. "That's me."

"Nice to meet you."

"And you. We'll have to get to know each other."

Joshua elbowed Sean in the ribs. His cousin was incorrigible. He met Stella's gaze and shook his head while wondering how much she'd told her cousin about his. But Elizabeth seemed unphased by Sean's brazenness, and simply replied that it would be nice to spend some time together.

"We could catch up tonight if you have nothing else planned."

Joshua glared at him. "That's enough, Sean." He turned to Elizabeth. "I apologise for my cousin."

She shrugged. "It's okay. No harm done."

"Come on, Liz. We'd better get going." Stella linked her arm through her cousin's, gave a nod, and then walked back towards the Jeep. Before they made it, another vehicle, a Toyota Hilux ute, approached from the other direction and stopped abruptly, sending a cloud of dust into the air. The door opened, and Julian jumped out, his face red as he stormed towards Joshua and Sean.

"I just got back from town, and I've been stewing on this the whole way back."

Joshua narrowed his eyes. "What are you talking about?"

Julian poked him in the chest. "There's word going around that you had indecent dealings with a guest."

Joshua stood up to him. "That's not true. Where did you hear that?"

"None of your business. It's the damage your misdemeanours will do to our good name that is." Julian stepped closer. "You were warned. Both of you. But you've abused your position. I've got a good mind to sack you both."

"There's no need. We quit. Come on, Sean. Let's get out of here." Joshua seethed. How dare Julian accuse him of something he hadn't done. Sean might have taken advantage of some of the girls, but he hadn't. Not even that girl who'd come onto him recently. Then the penny dropped. It must have been her getting revenge because he wouldn't pay her attention. Curses fell from his mouth as he pulled Sean away.

"You can't leave yet. There's a drive in two days," Julian stated.

"Watch us."

Joshua grabbed his keys and jumped into the driver's side of his own Hilux. As Sean climbed in the other side, Joshua started the engine and took off, spinning the wheels and sending a spray of red dust and gravel into the air. Passing Stella and Elizabeth, who were standing by the Jeep with open mouths, he gulped. He didn't know they were still there. But whatever. She was too good for him, anyway.

STELLA HADN'T HEARD all that had been said between Joshua and Julian, but she'd heard enough to know that this was serious. And the way Joshua sped off worried her. He wasn't in a good frame of mind to be driving in the growing darkness. Anything could happen. Cattle could be on the track, kangaroos were a danger at this time of night, and the road was rough and winding. She prayed he'd slow down and come to his senses. She was even tempted to go after him.

Aware that this wasn't a good thing for her cousin to see, although Elizabeth had witnessed it and there was nothing that could undo that, she motioned for her to stay back while she spoke with Julian.

By the tension in his jaw, it seemed that Joshua's reaction had taken him by surprise, too. She stood before him and studied him. It wasn't her place to tell her boss off, but at that moment, she agreed with Joshua. He was a jerk. "That went well," she said.

His shoulders slumped as he expelled a heavy breath. "No, it didn't. I should have handled it better."

"You push each other's buttons."

"Seems that way."

"What are you going to do?"

"Wait for them to come back."

She angled her head. "Do you think they will? I don't."

He let out a heavy sigh. "They've got nowhere else to go."

"I'm not so sure about that."

He shrugged. "I guess we'll see. I'm sorry you witnessed that. I didn't know you were there. It was unprofessional of me."

Her voice softened. "Things happen."

"Well, anyway. I'm sorry."

"It's not me you need to apologise to." She kept her voice even. "You may well have just lost your brother."

His jaw clenched tighter, but his eyes flickered.

"He and Sean are the only two who can do the drives."

He blew out a breath and raked his hand across his hair. "They'll come back."

"And if they don't?"

"I'll figure something out."

"Okay. I need to go. My cousin's in the car."

His face paled. She didn't tell him that Elizabeth had witnessed the whole scene. There was no need to embarrass him further.

She turned and headed back to her car.

"Are you okay?" Elizabeth asked once she was seated.

"No. I think Joshua's left for good."

"Oh dear."

CHAPTER 18

$\mathcal{M}$aggie gazed down at her tiny grandson and smiled. At two weeks, Oliver had begun to fill out, but he was still so small that he fitted easily along her forearm. Serena had brought him home a week before and was adjusting well to motherhood, just like Maggie said she would. David was doing a superb job supporting her, often getting up and sitting with her while she fed Oliver at three-hourly intervals during the night. David had also been doing most of the cooking, although Maggie always offered to help.

During the two weeks she and Frank had been in Darwin, they'd spent time with Jeremy and Emma, Maggie's son and daughter-in-law, and the two grandchildren, Sebastian and Chloe. Jeremy had filled her in on the latest with Cliff, her ex-husband and his dad. She almost didn't want to know, and she hadn't wanted to ask Serena, but when Jeremy told her that he'd been formally diagnosed with bipolar disorder, most likely triggered when the young girl he'd hit with his car died, her heart softened. He *had* been her husband for over thirty years, after all, and even though he'd been unfaithful, he was still her children's father and the thought of him having psychotic episodes grieved her. He was on medication and would soon be moved to the regular jail where he would serve a minimum of three years for manslaughter. Such a fall from grace for a man who'd once been a high-profile politician. *Pride goes before destruction, a haughty spirit before a fall.* But God still loved him, and Maggie prayed that while Cliff was in jail with copious amounts of time on his hands, he would consider his relationship with the Lord and humble himself before his Maker.

They'd caught up with Frank's sister and brother-in-law, Bethany and Graham, who'd taken them out for a day trip on their boat, and they'd enjoyed dinner at their favourite restaurant in Darwin, Pearls, a rare treat these days. They also went to church twice, and Maggie, in particular, delighted in being in God's house. The worship times had brought a tear to her eye and a song to her heart. The sermons had been uplifting, and she came away feeling renewed in her spirit.

She was more determined than ever to attend church as often as possible when they returned to Goddard Downs. It was so easy to go in Darwin since the church was only a ten-minute drive from David and Serena's apartment. It was a totally different matter to get to the church in Kununurra from Goddard Downs, especially in the rainy season when the only mode of transport was helicopter. Even in the dry season, it was a seven-hour round trip by car.

Maggie had asked Frank why they couldn't take the helicopter in the dry season, but he'd looked at her with a blank expression. She gathered it simply wasn't done although it made sense to her. The times they'd been, they stayed with Frank's other sister, Sarah, and her husband, Mick. It was also a chance for Frank to catch up with his elderly mother, Mrs. Mary, who lived with them. Maggie enjoyed the time they spent there, and she didn't mind the drive there and back, either, since it was time spent with Frank.

Oliver was just about asleep in her arms. Frank and David were having a long conversation on the balcony, and Serena was resting. Maggie knew she should put Oliver into his bassinet, but the time with him was too short, so she settled into the soft couch and closed her own eyes as she held him tight.

OUT ON THE BALCONY, Frank sat with his legs crossed while he answered the questions about Goddard Downs that David peppered him with. David was a firefighter, and his interest in Goddard Downs puzzled Frank until David mentioned that he was considering his employment options now he was a father. "I don't think Serena's too happy about me fighting raging fires anymore."

"I can understand that. It's a high-risk occupation."

"It is." A nerve in David's neck twitched as he leaned forward. "I...I don't suppose there'd be a job at Goddard Downs?"

Frank was momentarily lost for words. He liked David but was unsure what work he could do on the station. He hadn't been raised on the land, and Frank's thoughts immediately turned to Olivia's husband, Nathan, who'd struggled to adapt when the young couple had made the move from Darwin to help out after Esther died. "I'm not sure, David. As you know, I'm not in charge anymore, so I'd have to talk to the others, in particular, Julian, to see if there'd be any openings."

David nodded. "I understand. It was a longshot."

"How would Serena feel about leaving the city, especially with the motivational talks she's thinking of doing?"

"I haven't mentioned it to her yet. I thought I'd run the idea by you first. If it was an outright no, then it would be pointless discussing it. And she can do the talks wherever she is. Schools pay big money to have someone like her address their students."

David was right. There was plenty of scope for motivational talks in and around Kununurra where many of the youth seemed to have lost their way. "But she might not want to move."

"Since the blast, and now having had Oliver, she's a different person. The old Serena would never have considered living on a cattle station, but I think the new one might. Plus, I think she'd appreciate being closer to her mother."

Frank grimaced. "That's my fault."

David chuckled. "It's okay. One of you had to move."

"Yes. Fortunately for me, Maggie was happy to put her hand up. But it's come at a cost, because I know she misses her family."

David's countenance fell.

"I'm sorry, Dave. You must be feeling the loss of yours at the moment. That was thoughtless of me."

"It's okay. My aunt and cousins have all been supportive,

but you're right, I would have loved my mum to see her grandson."

Uncrossing his legs, Frank leaned forward and met David's gaze. "I've learned that it's no use dwelling on what can't be. We all suffer loss. It's part of life, and although it's important to grieve, eventually we have to let go and enjoy the people God has placed in our lives now."

David blew out a breath. "You're right. I'm so glad for Jeremy and Emma. They're like a brother and a sister to me."

"And it would be hard to leave them, I'd imagine."

"Yes."

"I think we should pray about what God wants you to do. Maybe He'll lead you to Goddard Downs, but maybe He has something else in store for you."

David nodded. "I've been praying, but I don't have any clear direction yet."

"Sometimes the answer comes in a way you least expect. You just have to exercise patience. Would you like me to pray for you now?"

David smiled. "That would be great."

Frank leaned closer and placed his hand lightly on David's shoulder as he closed his eyes. "Heavenly Father, thank You for this young man and for his desire to look after his family. Lord, as he considers his employment options, I ask that You'll guide and lead him to whatever it is You have in store for him, and I ask that You'll bless him and Serena and little Oliver abundantly as they live for You. Thank You for the things You've taught them and the way You're opening doors for Serena to share her story with young people. To show them that life doesn't end just because of a setback or two, regardless of how big those setbacks are. Lord, we entrust our lives to You, and ask that You use us to extend Your Kingdom here on earth. In Your precious Son's name. Amen."

"Amen," David echoed, at the same time as Frank's phone rang.

Frank pulled the phone from his pocket, asked David to excuse him, and then stood up and answered it while he leaned on the railing. It was Olivia, and she sounded on edge.

"Dad, sorry to interrupt your holiday, but Joshua's missing."

A chill ran down Frank's spine. "What do you mean?"

"He stormed out two days ago with Sean, and they haven't been heard from or seen since."

"Let me guess. An argument with Julian?"

"Yes. I wasn't there, but I've heard it was heated."

"Those boys," Frank muttered under his breath, the corner of his mouth twisting with exasperation. "Does anybody have any idea where they might be?"

"No. His phone's turned off and he hasn't made contact."

"I'll come home."

"No, Dad. Don't do that. We only wanted to let you know, that's all. Don't cut your trip short. We don't want you to do that."

"How's Julian?"

"Quiet. If Joshua doesn't come back by tomorrow, he's going to cancel the drive that starts the following day."

"Why doesn't he do it himself?"

"Dad…"

"I know." He didn't say it, but he thought it might do Julian good to get his hands dirty for once. "Okay. Let me know if you hear anything or if you need me to come home."

"I will. Sorry to be the bearer of bad news."

"It had to happen. The fuse between those two was lit a long time ago."

"I know. I feel like banging their heads together."

"You and me both. I just hope Joshua doesn't come to any harm."

"That's the worry. Stella saw him drive off and she said he was mad. We've scoured the entire road into town but there's no sign of an accident."

"Well, that's good news. My guess is that he's gone to ground somewhere."

"They didn't take anything. Just what was in his truck, which probably wasn't much."

"He's resourceful. He'll survive."

"I hope so."

After ending the call, Frank stared across the bay, his heart heavy. He'd not had the chance to have that talk with Joshua, and now it might be too late.

But blessed is the one who trusts in the Lord, whose confidence is in Him. They will be like a tree planted by the water that sends out its roots by the stream. It does not fear when heat comes; its leaves are always green. It has no worries in a year of drought and never fails to bear fruit.

Lord, be with Joshua, Frank prayed silently. *You know where he is, and what state his mind is in. Keep him safe and bring him home. And please work in both Julian and Joshua's hearts and let them resolve the differences between them, once and for all.*

Later that afternoon, Frank suggested that he and Maggie take a walk along the waterfront. As they strolled hand-in-hand, he told her about Joshua and that he felt he should go home. "But you stay, my love. Serena needs you."

"No, she doesn't. She's coping amazingly well, and she has David. I want to go with you." When she looked up at him, he could see the determination in her eyes. "Your problems are my problems now," she said, "and besides, we can always come back. There's still a few weeks before the rainy season begins."

Lifting her hand to his lips, he kissed it gently. What a treasure he'd found in Maggie. Love for her flooded his heart as he gave thanks to the Lord once again for bringing her into his life.

CHAPTER 19

*J*oshua stared at his phone as he downed another beer. He'd turned it off two days earlier and hadn't turned it back on. There'd be messages, but he didn't want to hear them. But then again, he did. Sean had taken him to this dive in Kununurra, a house devoid of rules, where people came and went all hours of the day and night, that reeked of alcohol, stale cigarettes, and dope. Joshua didn't smoke, nor did he take drugs, despite Sean and everyone else offering them to him. *They'll make you feel better, mate. Forget about your brother, dude. He sounds like a useless jerk.* And on it went. And went. And went. His head hit the floor with a bang. He groaned. What was he doing here?

Sometime later, he woke to Sean shaking him. "Come on, cuz, we need to go out."

"What for?"

"There are two spots left in the rodeo. We need to get them before anyone else does."

"I don't feel like it."

"Don't give me that crap. This is what we've been wanting. Get yourself up and we'll get outta here." Sean grabbed his arm and pulled him to his feet. Joshua stumbled and almost fell. His head thumped like a jackhammer. "Did you spike my drink?"

"Nope. But you drank enough to wipe yourself out."

Joshua groaned again. He was getting too old for this. "Give me a moment." He stumbled into the bathroom and puked into the toilet bowl. After a few moments, he splashed his face with cold water and studied himself in the mirror. What a wreck. His eyes were bloodshot, his hair a mess. He reached into his back pocket for his comb. Fixing his hair didn't improve his appearance much, but at least he didn't look like a homeless person.

But that's what he was. Homeless. He could never go back. Not ever. But he couldn't stay here. Sean might be happy to live in a dive like this, but he couldn't. He'd do the rodeo, make some money and then hit the road. Drive as far as his money would take him. He slumped against the wall. Who was he kidding? The only person he had a problem with was Julian. But how could he go home while his brother was there?

But I say to you who hear, love your enemies, do good to those who hate you, bless those who curse you, pray for those who mistreat you. Whoever hits you on the cheek, offer him the other also; and whoever takes away your coat, do not withhold your shirt from him either.

No. He didn't want to hear that. It was no good. He straightened and splashed his face again and then headed out to join Sean. "Come on cuz, let's go."

FRANK AND MAGGIE arrived home the following day just as the family was sitting down to dinner. They'd driven all day, and although tired, were eager to get an update on Joshua. There was none.

"We've all tried calling him, but his phone's still turned off," Olivia said.

"Someone has to go looking for him," Frank said as he sat down.

"Agreed," Olivia replied. "What do you suggest?"

Frank cast his gaze around the table. To his left, Janella sat beside Julian who was unusually quiet, his lips pursed as though none of this was his fault. Opposite were Olivia and Nathan, and to his right, beside Maggie, sat Stella. Frank thought it strange that she should be at the family dinner table but shrugged it off. Maggie had told him several times she thought something was going on between Stella and his youngest. He hadn't seen it for himself, but perhaps she was right. The younger grandchildren had already eaten and were in bed. The older two, Caleb and Sasha, were sitting quietly between Stella and Olivia.

"Okay. Two of us need to look after the drives that are already booked. Best not to take any new bookings. I'm guessing tomorrow's has been cancelled?"

Olivia shook her head. "I tried to cancel it, but the people weren't cooperative. Stella and Nathan are geared up to do it."

Frank's brow shot up. "Really?" He thought that an odd pairing. He faced his eldest son. "Why aren't you doing it, Julian?"

A look of horror crossed his face. "Me? Go on a drive?"

"Why not? You can ride."

"But I'm needed here."

Frank stared at his son. When had he become so haughty? "I think you and Nathan should do it together. Stella is needed here more than you over the next few days."

Julian's gaze narrowed as he folded his arms and slunk down in his seat. "Fine."

"Good. Janella and Liv, you two should call anyone who might know Joshua's whereabouts."

The two women nodded.

"That leaves Stella, Maggie and me. I'd like to go into town and look for him."

"Dad, he could be anywhere by now. I doubt he'll still be in town," Olivia said.

"You might be right, but I can't sit here and do nothing."

Stella cleared her throat and leaned forward. "It might not be my place to say anything, but I think going after him won't work. He needs to come back in his own time."

Frank studied her. "And how do you know this?"

"We've...we've known each other for a while. We met at the rodeo in Alice."

"I knew it," Maggie said quietly.

"Has he been in contact with you?" Frank asked.

"No."

"But you're in a relationship?"

"Not really, but we were talking a lot before he left."

Julian pinned her with a narrowed gaze. "About me?"

Stella visibly gulped. "Some. He wasn't happy about the way you treated him."

"He needs to grow up."

Her eyes blazed. "No, you need to give him credit for his abilities. He's great at what he does. You just don't see it."

There was stunned silence at the table. Maggie grabbed Frank's hand and rubbed it.

"And you do?" Julian asked in a measured tone.

"Yes," Stella replied. "He's great with the guests, but not in the way you accused him of. From what I've seen, he's helpful and patient."

"And you've been here…how long?"

"Long enough."

"Okay. Enough, you two." Frank straightened. "Julian, you and I need to talk. And we all need to pray for Joshua and Sean's safety, and for wisdom to know what to do. We won't go into town looking for him. You're right." He looked at Olivia. "He could be anywhere by now. Darwin, Broome, Perth. Who knows."

"God does," Maggie said quietly.

Frank nodded. "Yes, He does. And I think we should pray." He held out his hands and his expression left no room for anyone to ignore him. He might not be in charge of the station anymore, but he was still head of this family.

After they all joined hands, Frank bowed his head and began. "Lord God, forgive us our sins, which are many. Forgive us for the times when we've been selfish and have put our own needs and desires before those of our brothers and sisters. For the times when we've said harsh words, allowed wrong thoughts to control our actions, when we haven't loved in the way You've instructed us to. Lord, I pray that You'll heal this rift between Julian and Joshua. That You'll reach deep inside their hearts and convict them of their need of humility. The same humility that Your Son showed when He humbled Himself and became a man when He didn't have to. When He gave up everything He had with You because of His love for us. Love we don't deserve. Lord, we bow in Your presence and seek Your blessing on this family. Bind us together with Your love, and look after Joshua and Sean, wherever they are. We pray these things in Jesus' precious name. Amen."

Subdued amens sounded around the table.

"Now, let's eat this meal before it gets cold," Frank said.

Instead of picking up his silverware, Julian pushed his chair back, stood, and asked to be excused. Janella stood and grabbed his hand. Their gazes locked while everyone watched. He told her to sit down. She sat and an uncomfortable quiet filled the room. Witnessing discord between husband and wife was never comfortable, and worse when children were present. Frank glanced at Caleb. He was blinking faster than normal, behaviour he exhibited often following Esther's death. Frank hadn't noticed it for some time. His heart went out to the boy as his annoyance with Julian grew. He prayed that God would get through to his eldest son and that he would return and apologise to everyone at the table, especially his wife and children. For a grown man who considered himself a Christian, his behaviour was unacceptable, and his attitude towards Joshua stunk. Frank had a good mind to take back management of the station. It was a pity that Julian was a born manager and was doing a sterling job in every area other than managing his own brother.

He leaned over and spoke quietly to Janella. "I'll go after him shortly."

She nodded, and for the first time in all the years he'd known her, tears flooded her eyes.

~

JULIAN HEADED OUTSIDE. His heart hammered, and his breathing was ragged. How dare Dad point the finger at him! He wasn't to blame for his brother's poor choices. It was Joshua who needed to get his act together, not him.

He jumped into his truck and sped off. He had no destination in mind, he simply needed space. He thumped the steering wheel with his hand and didn't see the bullock standing in the middle of the road until it was too late. He hit the brakes and skidded, but it was like hitting a brick wall at full speed. The impact flipped the truck and as it rolled down the small embankment, his mind went blank.

~

EVERYONE DROPPED their silverware and stared at each other. As if in slow motion, one by one, they stood and sprinted outside.

Janella reached the crash site first. Julian's truck was on its roof down a small embankment to the side of the road. The tyres were still spinning and steam hissed from the radiator.

"Stay back," Frank yelled. He grabbed Janella and pulled her away. "Stay with the children. Nathan, come with me."

"Frank, be careful!" Maggie called out.

He turned and looked at his wife. Her face was distraught. "I will," he called back. "Get the first-aid kit and stretcher."

Nathan joined him and they sprinted to the vehicle. It was unlikely the diesel would ignite, but Julian could be in a bad way. He could even be dead. Frank glanced at the bullock writhing on the ground which Stella was already attending. No doubt it would be euthanised.

He and Nathan clambered down the embankment towards the truck. Memories of another accident he'd rescued Julian from flitted through his mind. This one was worse. Julian's neck was at a strange angle and blood pooled around his head. It didn't look good. "Is there a pulse?" Frank asked as Nathan leaned in and felt Julian's neck.

Nathan shook his head, but then said, "Wait. I can feel a faint one."

Frank breathed a sigh of relief. While there was life, there was hope. "We've got to get him out."

"I'm not sure how."

"Carefully."

Julian hadn't been wearing his seatbelt, and now, with the vehicle on its roof, he was sprawled against it. "Let's try to open the door," Frank said.

Together, he and Nathan tried to move it, but it wouldn't budge. "We'll need to go in through the front." The windscreen had smashed, and the gap was large enough for Nathan to climb through.

"How's he look?" Frank asked.

"I need something to stop the bleeding."

Frank clambered back up the small incline and called for Maggie to bring the first-aid kit. Janella, Olivia and the children were all huddled together, sobbing.

Maggie hurried over. "What do you need?"

"Rags. Something to stop the bleeding."

She rummaged through the kit and handed him a wad of bandages. "Try these."

Frank took them.

"How does he look?" Maggie asked quietly.

"He's alive. Just."

"Praise God. Is there anything I can do?"

"Pray."

She nodded and walked off to sit on a log where he knew she would be deep in intercession.

He clambered back down and passed the wad of bandages to Nathan.

Nathan applied the wad to the gash and secured it with his shirt which he'd ripped off. Together, he and Frank carefully manoeuvered Julian from the vehicle and placed him on the stretcher. "We need to get him to the hospital," Frank said to Janella who'd suddenly appeared at their side and grabbed Julian's hand.

"I'll fire up the helicopter," she said, urgency in her voice.

"No, call the Flying Doctor. None of us are in a good way to be flying," Frank replied.

"Let me go with him." Caleb stepped forward and stood by his mother's side, his face distraught.

Janella wrapped her arms around him. "Sweetheart, I'm not sure that's a good idea."

He nodded and then burst into tears.

"He'll be okay, Caleb." She hugged him tighter and rubbed his back as she met Frank's gaze over her son's shoulder.

"But what if he's not?" Caleb sobbed.

The boy's distress tore at Frank's heart. Memories of Esther's death would no doubt have been revived. "He'll be okay, son. You'll see." Frank glanced at Maggie who was deep in prayer and desperately hoped he was right.

CHAPTER 20

A dull ache of foreboding weighed heavily on Janella as she stood by her husband's hospital bed. She tried to convince herself that Julian wasn't dying, but despite everyone else's bravado and confidence, she knew he was slipping away. Although his outward injuries would heal, the internal ones were so bad that even the doctors held little hope.

The force of the collision with the bullock and the subsequent rollover had pushed his ribs into his lungs, crushing them, and he'd died twice while being airlifted to Kununurra Hospital. His heart had been bruised and he'd suffered massive internal bleeding. Following ten hours of surgery, he was drifting in and out of consciousness.

The Royal Flying Doctor plane had arrived within thirty minutes of the call being made. She'd flown with him to the hospital while the rest of the family drove. Sarah and Mick had opened their home and made up beds for them all, but no one could sleep. Other than the children, who'd stayed with Sarah, they were all there, standing around Julian's bed. But one person was missing. Joshua.

While the hours ticked away during Julian's surgery, they'd all made numerous phone calls, to no avail. No one had any clue as to Joshua's whereabouts. Janella prayed he would be found in time, but time was running out.

Julian moaned and his eyes flicked open briefly.

"Hey, hon. How are you doing?" With one hand, she smoothed his forehead while squeezing his hand with the other. "We're all here."

His eyes opened again, and his gaze slowly travelled around the bed. "Josh…" His eyes closed again as his voice trailed off.

Janella looked at Olivia. They had to find him.

"I'll keep trying." Olivia brushed her eyes, gave Janella a hug and pulled out her phone.

Letting go of Julian's hand, Janella turned and stepped into Frank's arms and sobbed.

STELLA WAS HOLDING the fort at Goddard Downs. Following the family's departure, instead of returning to her unit, she'd stayed at the homestead, and after cleaning up the dining room and kitchen, she'd gotten down on her knees and prayed.

Although she was a vet, she knew enough about medicine to know that Julian's chances of survival were slim. The medical team had acted swiftly, but she'd seen the looks on their faces and read between the lines. As they were loading him onto the plane, they'd had to resuscitate him. The mood had been sombre amongst everyone as the plane took off into the night sky. Soon after, they'd stood together and prayed for Julian. And for Joshua, whom they all knew needed to be found in case Julian didn't make it.

Then they all left. She wasn't part of the family. She was only an employee, although she felt more than that. The Goddard family had become more than her employers. They'd become her friends, and now, with the house empty apart from her and Elizabeth, she felt alone.

All night, they'd interceded on Julian's behalf, pleading with God to spare his life. Sometime during the endless night, she had a dream, or possibly a vision, she wasn't sure which, of Julian standing before God, and God asking if he was ready to face judgment. Julian had said no. He needed to make amends with his brother first. Stella had woken to fresh tears on her cheeks and peace in her heart. Somehow, God had this. Whether Julian lived or died was in God's hands, but while he lived, God was doing a work in his heart.

She fell asleep in the wee hours of the morning and only woke when her phone beeped. Daylight streamed in through the living room curtains. She quickly grabbed her phone and checked the time. It was seven a.m., and the message was from Joshua.

She blinked and then read it.

I'm sorry.

That was all. But it meant he was alive; and his phone was on. She quickly dialled the number and prayed he'd answer.

He did. Although he was on the line, he said nothing. Then she heard sobbing.

"Joshua, are you there?"

He sniffed. "Yes." His voice was barely audible.

"Have you heard the news?"

He sniffed again. "About Julian?"

"Yes."

"Is it true?" he asked.

"Yes. He's in the hospital. He had an accident. Have you spoken to Janella?"

"No. There were messages. Lots of them."

"You have to see him. Where are you?"

"In town."

"Kununurra?" she asked, hopeful that's where he was, and not Darwin, or Perth or somewhere else far away.

"Yes."

She beathed a sigh of relief. "Are you okay?"

He didn't reply for a moment, but then he uttered a faint, "No."

Stella's heart constricted as she imagined all sorts of things. "What do you mean?"

"I...I got beat up."

She stifled a groan. She didn't want to know how it had happened, but guessed he must have gotten into a drunken argument with someone. Although it was morning, his words were slurred. "Are you injured?"

There was another moment of silence before he replied, "No."

"Is Sean with you?"

"Yes."

"Is he awake?"

"No."

He was probably as drunk as a skunk and of no use to Joshua, anyway. "Where are you, Joshua?"

More silence. She prayed he hadn't fallen asleep. "Joshua. Are you still there?"

"Yes."

"Do you know where you are?"

"In a house."

"Do you have an address?" She waited eagerly for his answer.

"No, but it's near a pub."

"Which pub?"

"The Grand."

"What does the house look like?"

"A dive."

Stella knew the type and hated to think of Joshua living in a place like that. "Okay. I'm going to call your dad and he'll come and find you. Joshua, this is important. Are you with me?"

"Yes."

"Go and freshen up. You need to be awake and sober when you see Julian."

"Why?"

"Because he's dying."

The line went dead. Stella blew out a breath and dialled Frank's number. He answered on the first ring.

"I've found him," she said.

JOSHUA STRUGGLED to keep his eyes open, but the words rang in his ears. *Julian was dying. Dad was coming.* He pushed to his feet and staggered to the bathroom, puked into the toilet bowl, and then fell into the shower. He reached up and turned the water on, and after several minutes, he felt mildly human. As he took some deep breaths, the reality of what was happening hit him.

Had he caused Julian's accident? If not directly, indirectly? Had their feud caused his brother to act erratically, just as it had him? The past few days had been a nightmare. Sean had gone crazy and taken him along for the ride. Joshua should have refused to go with him, but Sean wanted to celebrate their acceptance into the circuit in the only way he knew. By drinking. His stomach convulsed and he puked again. How could he go to the hospital and face his family?

His phone rang. When he glanced at it, his dad's name flashed on the screen. A shudder ran up Joshua's spine. How could he talk to him? But he had to. He'd not live with himself if Julian died before he got there. They might not see eye to eye, but Julian was his brother. He answered it. "Dad."

"Joshua."

At the sound of his father's voice, tears sprang to his eyes. "I'm sorry," he choked.

"It's alright, son. Whatever you've done, it's alright. Maggie and Nathan will come for you. I can't leave Julian."

"Is he… is he…"

"Dying?"

"Yes." He could barely get the word out.

"It's not looking good."

Joshua sucked in a breath. "Is it my fault?"

"No. Julian chose to drive without a seatbelt. That's not your doing."

Relief flooded him. "Okay. I'll get dressed and wait out front."

"Good. They'll be there in ten minutes."

"Okay."

After the call ended, Joshua dried himself but he had nothing to wear. Since leaving Goddard Downs, he'd worn the same clothes, day in and day out, and they were filthy. He held up his jeans and shirt and the smell almost made him puke again. But there was no option. He couldn't go shopping. Rummaging through the bathroom cabinet, he found a bottle of cologne. That would have to do. He put his shirt on and then his jeans before spraying them liberally. He grabbed a cloth, and after dampening it, gave his jeans a once over. Not great, but it would have to do.

He quickly combed his hair and returned to the living room to find his boots. They were on the floor where he'd collapsed. The socks could almost stand by themselves, but he had to put them on. At least the boots would cover them. Sean was snoring loudly on the floor. Two other dudes were out cold on the couch. Everywhere he looked were overflowing ashtrays, bong pipes, and empty beer bottles. How did he end up in a place like this?

Despite his throbbing head, he walked out the door and determined never to return. Looking up into the sky, he called out to God. *I'm sorry. I don't know how I got to this point. Show me the way home.*

CHAPTER 21

*M*aggie kept her eyes peeled for Joshua as Nathan inched his car along the streets around the Grand Hotel. Although Joshua and Julian weren't her biological sons, she'd come to love them as if they were her own offspring and her heart grieved for them both. Whatever had gone on between them, Joshua would be distressed to learn that Julian was dying, and she prayed silently that God would give her words that would comfort him. But first, they had to find him.

Kununurra, like many towns in the outback, had unsavoury areas that most people avoided. This was one of them. Rundown houses with long grass and broken gates lined each street. Empty beer bottles lay in the gutters. Emaciated dogs rummaged through rubbish bins. She was glad Frank wasn't here to see it. It would have grieved him even more than it grieved her to know that Joshua had been staying somewhere like this.

Three dark skinned children with large round eyes sat in the gutter and looked up as they drove past. "Who yer lookin' for, Missus?" one asked.

"A tall man with short, dark hair," Maggie replied out the window.

"Haven't seen no one like that."

"Okay. Thank you."

They continued on. Maggie didn't know Nathan well. In fact, until now, she'd not spent any time with him on her own, so it felt strange to be in a car with him looking for Joshua. But he was as keen as she was to find him. He'd taken a methodical approach, ensuring they didn't miss any street near the hotel. The description of the house they'd been given was of no help at all. All the houses near the hotel were dives.

"Only two streets left before we get into the better area," Nathan said as he turned left onto yet another street lined with rundown houses.

"There he is!" Maggie pointed ahead to a figure sitting in the gutter, staring at the ground.

As they approached, Joshua looked up, his face ashen. Pushing to his feet, he stood and waited for the car to stop.

Maggie and Nathan both jumped out. Maggie enveloped him in her arms. "It's so good to see you, Joshua."

As JOSHUA NODDED, a sense of shame flowed through him at having Maggie see him like this. But it felt so good to be hugged. He sucked in a breath and tried to steady his emotions. When she released him, Nathan gave him a quick hug. No doubt he was blaming Joshua for this mess. But Dad had said it wasn't his fault. "What...what happened?" he asked as Nathan helped him into the front seat of the car, seating him in the middle between him and Maggie.

"Julian stormed out during dinner. The truck hit a bullock and rolled," Nathan replied. "He wasn't wearing his seatbelt."

That might have been so, Joshua thought, but what made him storm out? It had to have been because of him, but he'd leave it for now. It didn't matter. "Is he really dying?"

Maggie took his hand. "He's in a bad way, Joshua. He's suffered massive internal bleeding and the doctors have only given him a slim chance of survival."

He shuddered inwardly as terrible regrets assailed him. He should have been more tolerant of Julian. Mum would have wanted that. She would have hated the way they'd been treating each other.

"It's my fault." He almost choked on the words.

"No, you can't blame yourself, Joshua. Julian's a grown man and is responsible for his own actions."

He sat quietly, and for the first time in many years, he prayed silently and asked God to save his brother and to forgive him for his own pigheadedness.

AFTER NATHAN PARKED, Maggie walked beside Joshua the whole way to the ICU. She knew he probably dreaded seeing everyone, especially his dad and Janella. If Julian died, Janella would be a widow, and the children will have lost their father. Although Maggie had assured Joshua this wasn't his fault, no doubt he was blaming himself. She couldn't imagine how he was feeling but prayed that God would wrap His comforting arms around him. They'd all been praying Julian would survive, but sometimes God didn't answer prayers in the way people wanted. Although it was hard to accept or understand, they all knew that if this was Julian's time to go, who were they to argue?

The ICU was on the ground floor of the small hospital. Questions had been asked as to whether Julian should have been taken to a larger hospital with more equipment, but time had been the determining factor, and the surgeon had assured them that Julian would receive the same treatment he'd receive elsewhere. They accepted that, and now, as the trio approached his ward, Maggie prayed that Julian had hung on long enough for Joshua to see him.

Pausing at the main doors, Maggie asked Joshua if he was okay.

He nodded, but said he'd like to go to the bathroom.

While she and Nathan waited for him to return, she sent Frank a text to let him know they were there and to ask how Julian was doing.

He replied that Julian was holding on, but that they'd sent for the children. She read between the lines. Janella and Frank had debated about whether Caleb and Sasha should be at their father's bedside. They weren't small children, but they'd already been emotionally scarred when their grandmother was swept away in the floods when they were young. Janella and Frank decided in the end that the decision would be left up to the children. They both decided they wanted to be there. Although it would be gut wrenching for them, Maggie believed it was the right decision. Death was part of the fabric of life, and although it was distressing for those left behind, for those who believed, death wasn't to be feared. Although Julian had his faults, he was a believer.

Joshua returned after several minutes. Maggie smiled at him. "Are you ready?"

"Not really."

She rubbed his back. "You'll be okay. We've been praying for you and you're stronger than you think."

Tears welled in his eyes. "Thank you."

She handed him a tissue, which he took. "Okay, let's do this," he said after drying his eyes.

She held his hand as they walked through the ward. Julian's cubicle was in the middle, and the curtains were pulled around his bed. As she parted them slowly, she caught Frank's gaze and nodded.

JOSHUA SWALLOWED hard as he entered the cubicle. Julian was lying on the bed, and apart from the drips and monitors, the breathing tube and the bandage on his head, he looked almost normal. It was hard to believe he might be dying. Maggie had told him that it was Julian's internal injuries that couldn't be seen that were the problem.

Everyone looked up and he felt he was under scrutiny. Janella was sitting beside Julian, holding his hand. Dad stood behind her with his hand resting on her shoulder. Olivia had her arm around his waist. They were all connected, and once again, Joshua felt like an outsider, like he didn't belong. But then they all reached out, and one at a time, hugged him, offering words of encouragement and love. He didn't deserve such treatment, but boy, did he appreciate it.

We were so worried about you. Good to see you, son. So glad you made it in time...

It was surreal. How could Julian be dying?

Janella motioned for him to sit on the seat beside the bed. They all stepped back and made way for Joshua to squeeze into the small space. He sat down and looked at Julian. "Will he hear me?" he asked of no one in particular.

"We're not sure, son," his dad replied. "But assume he will."

Joshua nodded. "Hey, big brother. What are you doing here? This wasn't meant to happen. I...I'm sorry for the way I treated you. I don't know why I let it continue for so long. Please forgive me. You don't have to do this, you know. You don't have to leave us." Tears welled in his eyes, and his chest tightened. This couldn't be happening. Without thinking, he took Julian's hand and was startled when he felt a slight squeeze. Julian had heard him.

The children arrived and Joshua stood to give them space. Several minutes later, the monitor beeped loudly. The crash team rushed in and tried to revive Julian, but as they watched from a distance, he slipped away and was pronounced dead at ten minutes past eight.

CHAPTER 22

The trip home was slow and solemn. Joshua requested that he accompany the hearse carrying Julian's body all the way from Kununurra to Goddard Downs, where the funeral was to be held that afternoon, on horseback. It was not a standard request. In fact, the funeral company had initially said no, but he insisted, and after much discussion, it was agreed that not only would he accompany the vehicle, but the whole family would.

They set off in the pale light of predawn. The eight horses Mick had borrowed for them followed the hearse at a walking pace as the procession headed out of town. The only sound was the clip-clopping of the horses' hooves on the road, and the soft purr of the vehicle.

Joshua rode up front with his father. Behind them, Janella was flanked by Caleb and Sasha, and behind them, Olivia, Nathan and Maggie brought up the rear.

When they reached the open road, they picked up the pace

to a slow trot, and as the miles slipped away, the group sang hymns of praise and worship. Filled with sorrow and regret over Julian's death, Joshua had been reluctant to join in, but as he listened to the others, he had the strong impression that God was saying to him, 'Joshua, I love you. No one is condemning or punishing you, and I don't either. Draw near to Me and I will give you peace.'

Although few of the songs were familiar, he joined in when he could, and peace slowly filled his heart, replacing the guilt he felt over his brother's death. By the time they reached Goddard Downs, he was ready to say goodbye to Julian.

Sarah and Mick had driven ahead and prepared a small outdoor chapel on the side of the hill overlooking the family cemetery and the plains below. Despite the long, slow ride, the procession continued past the homestead, not stopping until they reached the gathering on the hill.

Joshua dismounted first before helping Janella off her horse. While he was used to sitting in the saddle for hours on end, the ten hours had taken its toll on the others, including his dad. But no one complained. It was a ride they'd never forget, one that had forged a bond between them like nothing else had while Julian was alive. It was as if his death had made them all re-evaluate what was important, and Joshua now had clarity of heart and mind. He'd allowed both Sean and Julian to get under his skin, to cloud his focus, to unsettle him. But Goddard Downs was his home, and this was his family.

STANDING at the top of the hill, Stella watched the procession approach and then come to a stop. Although the news of Julian's death hadn't surprised her, it saddened her and she couldn't help the tears that formed in her eyes as she met Joshua's gaze after he dismounted his horse.

She wouldn't intrude on this intimate family event. She was there to help, but later, she would go to him and wrap her arms around him and tell him she was sorry. Death had the ability to crystalise what was important in life, and if he were still willing, she'd tell him she wanted to be more than friends, and that getting Indigo back was no longer a priority. Over the past few days, God had been nudging her heart as she went about her work, and she'd finally realised she'd placed a higher priority on getting the station back than on seeking Him. Nothing was more important than a right relationship with God. She knew that now, and she would trust Him with her future. If that future included Joshua Goddard, that would make her very happy.

She brushed her eyes and adjusted the chairs. Sarah and Mick had insisted that chairs be provided for the family after such a long ride. "They'll be physically and emotionally spent," Sarah had said.

Pastor Tim, the middle-aged pastor from the church in Kununurra, greeted the family one by one. Friends from neighbouring stations stood and nodded as the family acknowledged their presence before taking their seats.

Stella carried a tray containing glasses of water to the group, and as she walked along, she offered her condolences to each member. As her gaze briefly met Joshua's, she saw a depth in his eyes she hadn't seen before, and she knew that Julian's death had changed him.

The undertakers removed Julian's coffin from the hearse and set it on a simple timber frame between the seats and the small lectern where Pastor Tim stood. His gaze travelled over the assembled group before he addressed them.

"We're gathered together to bid farewell to Julian Francis Goddard. Julian's passing has left us all with a deep sense of sadness. He was a man in the prime of life. A husband, a father, a son, and he will be deeply missed by all. But we know that for those who love God, although death is a mystery, it is not to be feared. Jesus said, 'In My Father's house are many mansions; if it were not so, I would have told you. I go to prepare a place for you.' Julian is in that place now with the Father." Smiling warmly, Pastor Tim said, "Let us pray." He bowed his head and began. "Lord God, Creator of heaven and earth, we stand before You today in complete humility as we recognise Your sovereignty. Although our hearts are heavy and we don't understand why he was taken so early, we rejoice that Julian is now with You, and that one day, we will all be reunited. Bless and strengthen his family in their time of mourning. Let them hold on to Your steadfast love as they grieve the loss of their beloved Julian. In Your precious Son's name, we pray. Amen."

Olivia stood and walked to the lectern. Opening her Bible, she read from Romans chapter eight.

"Who shall separate us from the love of Christ? Shall trouble or hardship or persecution or famine or nakedness or danger or sword? As it is written: 'For your sake we face death all day long; we are considered as sheep to be slaughtered.' No, in all these things we are more than conquerors through Him who loved us. For I am convinced that neither death nor life, neither angels nor demons, neither the present nor the future, nor any powers, neither height nor depth, nor anything else in all creation, will be able to separate us from the love of God that is in Christ Jesus our Lord. Amen."

After she returned to her seat, Joshua rose and walked forward, and Stella's heart clenched. She knew how much emotion would be surging through him, and she prayed silently for him.

He paused and brushed his eyes with the back of his hand before he looked up and began. Unlike Olivia's controlled voice, his was broken. "I never thought I'd be standing here saying goodbye to my brother." He sniffed and visibly swallowed, his Adam's apple bobbing. "Julian and I had our differences, but he was still my brother. I regret that I let our grievances carry on for so long. In the days since he died, I've come to realise that life's too short to allow grievances, petty or otherwise, to mar our relationships with each other. I'd been hanging onto the belief that I was better than Julian, but that's not the case. God's given each of us all different abilities, and Julian was a great guy, responsible and steady, and he loved his family so much, he would have done anything for them. I remember when he and Janella started seeing each other when they were only teenagers, and how much in love he was with her. He thought the sun shone out of her. He still did. I'm not sure why we let our egos get in the way, and I sorely regret it, but my prayer and hope is that Julian's death will draw us closer as a family. That we'll put any differences aside and see the good in each other, and that we'll find practical ways to show our love and unity.

"Dad, Maggie, Janella, Caleb, Sasha, Olivia, and Nathan, I promise to be there for you always, and with God's help, to be the best person I can be, and to make our mother proud. That's all." Tears streamed down his cheeks. Janella and Olivia both rose and hurried to him, hugging him. Frank nodded, pride on his face, while Maggie squeezed his hand.

Blinking, Stella brushed tears from her cheeks.

Soon after, once Pastor Tim had prayed again and they'd sung Psalm Twenty-three, *The Lord's my Shepherd*, the men, including Mick and Graham, who'd come from Darwin for the funeral, and Caleb, lifted the coffin and carried it slowly to the family cemetery. The remaining family members followed behind, and then the others, including Stella, joined the group.

Oh, how she wanted to comfort Joshua as he stood beside Janella. As he bent down and picked up a handful of Goddard Downs soil and threw it on top of Julian's grave after it had been slowly lowered into the ground. As he bowed his head when Pastor Tim committed Julian's body and soul to the Lord.

He lifted his head and his gaze slowly searched those standing on the opposite side until it settled on hers. His eyes were full of pain, but also hope. She smiled, and when he smiled back, her heart beat a crescendo.

MAGGIE CARRIED a tray containing two mugs of tea and several chocolate chip cookies she'd found in her pantry onto the deck, where Frank was already seated. She was bone tired and her body ached, but she would never regret riding that distance with the family. It had been such a slow ride home, but God had used it in amazing ways, particularly with Joshua.

He and Frank had finally talked, and Maggie rejoiced greatly as the young man opened his heart, not only to his earthly father, but his Heavenly One.

"Here we are." She smiled as she placed the tray onto the table, and sitting beside Frank, slipped her hand onto his thigh and rested her head on his shoulder.

He put his arm around her shoulders and rubbed her upper arm gently as they gazed at the night sky. She honestly didn't mind if they fell asleep there. After the events of the past few days, although her heart was heavy and ached for her new family, she'd fallen deeper and deeper in love with her husband, and she never wanted to leave his side.

Dear friends, let us love one another, for love comes from God. Everyone who loves has been born of God and knows God. Whoever does not love does not know God, because God is love.

NOTE FROM THE AUTHOR

I hope you enjoyed "Slow Ride Home" and that the ending didn't shock you too much! The truth is, not one of us knows how long we have on this earth. Only God is privy to that information, and despite our desperate prayers that He save our loved ones when death is knocking on their door, sometimes He has other plans for them and for those of us left behind. Often times it's hard to accept it when our prayers aren't answered in the way we want them to be. We can start to doubt God's love and care for us, we can wallow in guilt for not having enough faith, and on it goes. But the reality is that God is sovereign, and we need to understand that. He's in charge, and He truly loves us and He knows what's best because he sees the bigger picture.

I know many of you would have wanted Julian to recover and for the brothers to make up, but I felt the Lord leading me to end this story in this way. Find out how the family copes with Julian's death in "Slow Dance at Dusk", Book 5 in A Sunburned Land Series, out now! Plus, you can read the first chapter below.

To ensure you don't miss any of my new releases, why not join my Readers' list (http://www.julietteduncan.-com/linkspage/282748)? You'll also receive a free thank-you copy of "Hank and Sarah - A Love Story", a clean love story with God at the center.

Enjoyed "Slow Ride Home"? You can make a big difference. Help other people find this book by writing a review and telling them why you liked it. Honest reviews of my books help bring them to the attention of other readers just like yourself, and I'd be very grateful if you could spare just five minutes to leave a review (it can be as short as you like) on the book's Amazon page.

Keep reading for your bonus chapter of "Slow Dance at Dusk".

Blessings,

Juliette

"Slow Dance at Dusk"
Chapter 1

Life had continued throwing curveballs at Joshua, but with Julian's death, he'd finally struck out. The games of his past were over. There was no looking back.

In the four months since his brother's body had been laid to rest in the family cemetery at Goddard Downs, life had fallen into a new routine. To the outsider, all might appear normal, but Julian's death echoed in the halls of the homestead and the hearts of all who lived there. Yet, despite the sadness, good had come.

The moment Joshua's gaze met Stella's at Julian's funeral, he knew everything between them was about to change. And it had. Their friendship had blossomed and transformed into something he'd never dreamed possible. She was no longer an unattainable desire of his heart, but someone willing to stand by his side as he battled his demons, of which there were plenty.

Facing the bitter, angry man he'd become hadn't been easy, but was necessary if he no longer wanted to drift. And that's what he wanted. He didn't want to go through life without direction or focus, chasing fleeting excitement that in the end meant nothing. He didn't want to be like his cousin Sean, but he couldn't become Julian, either. He had to be himself. But first, he had to find out who that was.

He'd once heard that the love of the right woman could change a man. He wasn't sure if that was true, but as he stood on the tarmac of the Kimberley Regional Airport helipad, gazing into Stella Martin's deep, brown eyes, he thought it could be. She'd entered his life by chance at a rodeo in Alice Springs several years earlier, and then returned to it recently when she came to Goddard Downs seeking work. Now, as the station's vet, she'd become more a part of his life than he ever imagined possible. It was almost as if she'd always been part of him.

"I wish I didn't have to go." She took hold of his hand as a gust of wind sent her blonde hair flying about her face. She brushed the strands back behind her ear with her other hand and smiled wistfully.

She was gorgeous, and the mere sight of her made Joshua's heart quicken. He squeezed her hand as a long breath left his lungs. "I wish you didn't either, but you have to. It's Christmas and your family needs you."

"I *could* go at the beginning of the year. I feel as if I'm abandoning you."

Her concern warmed his heart, and although he wanted her to stay at Goddard Downs for Christmas, he couldn't allow her to sacrifice that special time with her family. Since Julian's passing, Joshua had gained a new appreciation of family. His one regret was that it had taken him so long to arrive at this point. "I wouldn't want you to do that. This is the first time your entire family will be together for Christmas since before you were born. You can't miss that."

"I know, but I'm torn. Things between us are just beginning, and the rainy season is here, and the station needs every hand."

"The station can manage two weeks without you." He stepped forward and raised his hand to her cheek while gazing into her eyes. *But I'm not sure I can...* He cleared his throat. "And with regards to us, I'd say things are going just fine. Wouldn't you?"

She gave a smile that sent his pulse racing. Her smile

emboldened him, and he felt stronger, like he could do anything if she were beside him.

He who finds a wife finds a good thing and obtains favour from God.

He blinked. *A wife?* Before Stella, he'd never had a steady girlfriend, let alone considered marriage. But this wasn't the first time that thought had come to him since meeting her.

"Are you okay, Joshua?" She looked at him with enlarged eyes.

His brow furrowed and he swallowed hard. "What makes you think I'm not?"

Taking hold of his other hand, she squeezed both gently. "I know you're still carrying guilt over Julian's death, and that you're still mourning." Her gaze softened. "I'm here for you if you ever need to talk."

It wasn't what he was thinking, but she was correct. He hadn't spoken to anyone about the lingering guilt he carried over his brother's death. Everyone, even Janella, had assured him it wasn't his fault. No one blamed him, but he simply couldn't shake the feeling that if he hadn't been so hot-headed and blind when he'd rushed off to Kununurra, leaving the family in the lurch, then perhaps Julian wouldn't have gotten into that truck in such a state of mind and he'd still be alive.

"Joshua?" Stella squeezed his hands again. "I can see it in your eyes. Don't do that to yourself. What happened to Julian wasn't your fault. You know that. So did he."

Joshua nodded slowly. She was right. Julian knew. He remembered the feel of his brother's hand squeezing his as he lay in that hospital bed, connected to machines, barely hanging onto life. Joshua had made it to his bedside in time to ask for forgiveness and to say goodbye, but it was too late for them to ever be the brothers they should have been. So many wasted years. They'd caused such grief to their father and to their family. And to God.

He drew a deep breath and shook his head to push the memories away. "You should get going. You don't want to miss your flight."

"Are you chasing me away?" Stella's voice held a hint of amusement.

"I'd never do that." Stepping closer, he cupped her face with his hands and gazed into her eyes. "It took us long enough to get to this point."

She wrapped her arms around his waist and smiled. Although she was tall for a woman, he still towered over her by several inches.

"I'm going to miss you," she whispered, longing filling her voice.

"I already miss you," he replied. "But the sooner you go, the sooner you'll be back. I want you to enjoy this trip. Make the most of the time you have with your family. Make every second count."

She nodded. "Only if you promise to do the same."

"I promise." He lowered his mouth and brushed her lips gently before deepening the kiss. He couldn't bear the thought of being apart from her for two weeks, and when she finally stepped back, he felt the loss immediately.

"I'll call when I get to my parents' place," she said, picking up the small bag from the ground and hoisting it onto her back.

"I'll be waiting," he said, soaking in every inch of her.

She gave a quick smile and then walked away. If he wasn't mistaken, she had tears in her eyes.

As STELLA HEADED to the taxi stand, she stole several glances at Joshua. Although her lips still tingled from his kiss and the distinctive scent of his spicy cologne lingered in her nostrils, her heart felt as heavy as her feet.

Why was doing the right thing so hard? Spending Christmas with her family wasn't a chore, but if she were honest, she'd rather spend it at Goddard Downs. With Joshua.

Brushing the tear from her eye, she gave one last wave and hitched her bag higher. She'd packed lightly since she wouldn't be in Cootamundra long, just two weeks, and she had no special plans other than spending as much time with her family as she could. Some of her cousins on her mother's side she hadn't seen in years, and she was also keen to see first-hand how her parents were settling into their new home. Despite not wanting to go, she needed to.

Behind, the noise from the helipad as a helicopter landed was almost deafening as she crossed to where a taxi sat wait-ing. She greeted the driver, a middle-aged man of Middle Eastern appearance, and opening the back door, she stuffed her bag onto the seat before turning to give Joshua another wave. He was standing right where she'd left him, and he was so downright hot that the mere look of him made her knees go to jelly. Short dark hair, the smattering of whiskers on his chin, muscles rippling under his crisp white button-down shirt, sleeves rolled up and tucked into a pair of snugly fitted jeans.

When he raised a hand and smiled, she fought the temptation to grab her bag and run to him. *How had this happened?* Only five months earlier she'd been fighting the attraction, but now, having admitted their feelings for one another, it was as if there was no one else in the world who could match her so perfectly.

I'm going to miss you, Joshua Goddard. Lord, take care of him and the entire Goddard family while I'm away. May Your mercy and grace be upon them as they continue to mourn. May they see the light of Your love even in these difficult times, and may You show them the way forward.

She waved to Joshua one last time as the taxi drove off.

The Goddards would be well. They had faith in God and He would take care of them. Her family was the unknown quantity, and she had no idea what to expect when she arrived.

To continue reading "Slow Dance at Dusk" - http://www.julietteduncan.com/linkspage/1483023

Secrets and Sacrifice

A Highland Christmas

True Love Series

Tender Love

Tested Love

Tormented Love

Triumphant Love

Precious Love Series

Forever Cherished

Forever Faithful

Forever His

A Time For Everything Series

A mature-age Christian Romance series

A Time to Treasure

She lost her husband and misses him dearly. He lost his wife but is ready to move on. Will a chance meeting in a foreign city change their lives forever?

A Time to Care

They've tied the knot, but will their love last the distance?

A Time to Abide

When grief hovers like a cloud, will the sun ever shine again for Wendy?

A Time to Rejoice

He's never forgiven himself for the accident that killed his mother.

Can he find forgiveness and true love?

Transformed by Love Christian Romance Series

Because We Loved

A decorated Lieutenant Colonel plagued with guilt. A captivating widow whose husband was killed under his watch...

Because We Forgave

A fallen TV personality hiding from his failures. An ex-wife and family facing their fears...

Because We Dreamed

When dreams are shattered, can hope be restored?

Because We Believed

A single mom forging a new life. A handsome chaplain who steals her heart...

Billionaires with Heart Series

Her Kind-Hearted Billionaire

A reluctant billionaire, a grieving young woman, and the trip *that changes their lives forever...*

Her Generous Billionaire

A grieving billionaire, a devoted solo mother, and a woman determined to sabotage their relationship...

Her Disgraced Billionaire

A billionaire in jail, a nurse who cares, and the challenge that changes their lives forever...

Her Compassionate Billionaire

A widowed billionaire with three young children. A replacement nanny who helps change his life...

The Potter's House Books...

Stories of hope, redemption, and second chances. *The Homecoming*

Can she surrender a life of fame and fortune to find true love?

Blessings of Love

She's going on mission to help others. He's going to win her heart.

The Hope We Share

Can the Master Potter work in Rachel and Andrew's hearts and give them a second chance at love?

The Love Abounds

Can the Master Potter work in Megan's heart and save her marriage?

Love's Healing Touch

A doctor in need of healing. A nurse in need of love.

Heroes Of Eastbrooke Christian Suspense Series

Safe in His Arms

SOME SAY HE'S HIDING. HE SAYS HE'S SURVIVING

Under His Watch

HE'LL STOP AT NOTHING TO PROTECT THOSE HE LOVES. NOTHING.

Within His Sight

SHE'LL STOP AT NOTHING TO GET A STORY. HE'LL SCALE THE HIGHEST MOUNTAIN TO RESCUE HER.

Stand Alone Christian Romantic Suspense

Leave Before He Kills You

When his face grew angry, I knew he could murder…

The Madeleine Richards Series

Although the 3 book series is intended mainly for pre-teen/Middle Grade girls, it's been read and enjoyed by people of all ages. Here's what one reader had to say about it: *"Juliette has a fabulous way of bringing her characters to life. Maddy is at typical teenager with authentic views and actions that truly make it feel like you are feeling her pain and angst. You want to enter into her situation and make everything better. Mom and soon to be dad respond to her with love and gentle persuasion while maintaining their faith and trust in Jesus, whom they know, will give them wisdom as they continue on their lives journey. Appropriate for teenage readers but any age can enjoy."* Amazon Reader

ABOUT THE AUTHOR

Juliette Duncan is a USA Today bestselling author of Christian romance stories that 'touch the heart and soul'. She lives in Brisbane, Australia and writes Christian fiction that encourages a deeper faith in a world that seems to have lost its way. Most of her stories include an element of romance, because who doesn't love a good love story? But the main love story in each of her books is always God's amazing, unconditional love for His wayward children.

Juliette and her husband enjoy spending time with their five adult children, eight grandchildren, and their elderly, long-haired dachshund, Chipolata (Chip for short). When not writing, Juliette and her husband love exploring the wonderful world they live in.

Connect with Juliette:

Email: author@julietteduncan.com

Website: www.julietteduncan.com

Facebook: www.facebook.com/JulietteDuncanAuthor

Printed in Great Britain
by Amazon

77519583R00120